1984

WHEN 2 WORLDS COLLIDE

Category: Adult/Young Adult
Genre: Horror

Disclaimer:
This is a work of fiction. All characters, locations, and businesses
are purely products of the author's imagination and are entirely
fictitious. Any resemblance to actual people, living or dead,
or to businesses, places, or events is completely coincidental.

1984 When Two Worlds Collide by Jerome Sitko

ISBN: 978-1-7341459-1-5

1984

WHEN 2 WORLDS COLLIDE

JEROME SITKO

I dedicate this book to my two biggest fans- Bill and Helen Wainscott.
They also happen to be the parents of my soulmate, Renee.
Without both of your love and support, this book would not be possible.

CHAPTER 1

JUNE, 1984
DRUG DEN

The sun melts into the Chicago skyline and a light drizzle begins falling. The heat and sprinkling of rain only make the humidity worse and the already egged-on short tempers become shorter. Ryan is in the drug den getting ready to go out for another night of *recruiting* for Charlie. The lair is always dark and moldy from the lack of sunlight and the mood from its residents and victims match, dark and rotting. Ryan and the other psychopomps (undead), that Charlie affectionately calls his *grouplings*, have no trouble seeing in low or no light. It is one of the many perks of being a groupling, right up there with no-free-will. Usually, grouplings are weak-minded or drug-addicted vagrants that were duped into *Sheol*—Charlie's name for the hellish alternate world that parallels ours—tricked into living an endless life of servitude for Charlie. They yield their mind and body to Erebus (a council of evil demons) in an unceremonious ritual of death. When someone dies in Sheol, they will be resurrected and brought back in an evolved state of dead-but-not-dead. If they meet their demise in our world, or *Adamah* as Charlie calls it, it is permanent. Their physical bodies will become worm bedding in the earth's soil and their souls will either reunite with their loved ones in paradise or suffer in an eternal kiln, smoldering in pain. Their human recruits rely on the grouplings to help them navigate the interior of the building, but they still stumble and trip from the drugs affecting their equilibriums. The drug den is an abandoned three-story brick building with mattresses soaked in blood, urine, semen and vomit. Hypodermic needles litter the floor and the stench of sex and fear hang heavy in the air. Nearly every inch of any walls that are still standing as well as the boards covering the windows are 'tagged' with colorful but fading gang graffiti from a time when gangs ruled this part of town. Charlie owns this building now and this is one of his hubs to leap from Sheol to Adamah. His grouplings work Chicago's inner city, bringing him fresh recruits to build his forces.

The steel door at the rear of the building is the conduit between the two worlds. When Charlie or his grouplings cross the threshold, they are in Adamah where their powers are limited, but most importantly where if you die you remain dead. This is why Charlie rarely ventures across this or any of the portals; death is eternal. His powers are limited and he feels vulnerable and insecure like when he was alive…human again.

Charlie hates what his former self represents. Before being converted by Erebus, he was an insecure introvert that preyed on women and feared men. He was an astute serial rapist and killer who officially is credited with seven murders in the states of Washington and Oregon. Only he knows the real truth and the number is in the thirties. Charlie can remember every young girl's face, body type, and that one thing, the *IT* factor, that he could not resist. It could be anything; how she smiled, a birthmark, even how she styled her hair, whatever it was that made Charlie tingle down under and report to his brain, *that's the one.* He kept every one of them locked away in picture palaces in his mind. When he wanted gratification, he would take a stroll through what he called *Skid Row* and visit them. If the FBI did not discount him as an obtuse social leper, they would have discovered the other twenty-three victims. He allowed them to incorrectly profile him and relished in their incompetence, but he secretly wanted to be discovered so he could take credit where credit was due. He felt he deserved the notoriety of a Ted Bundy, but he wasn't going to just hand it over to the imbeciles and let them get the glory. Charlie is omni-powerful in Sheol and can satisfy every sadistic whim that pops in his head, so none of that matters now. Victims (grouplings) are in an endless supply and he can create or recreate any nightmare. Yes, life in Sheol is great for Charlie and he wants to keep it that way, but to do so, he has to finish what he started. He failed to capture Lance and Jeremy and use their mystical blood to syncretize Adamah and Sheol the last time. Lance and Jeremy's ancestors were so evil and vile a spell was cast on them when they were captured centuries ago. Their blood is the only blood that can merge the two worlds. It was thought the bloodline was extinct until Lance and Jeremy were born. Charlie knows Erebus won't give him another opportunity, but he has an ace card: Ryan.

———

Ryan opens the steel door with his partner Amy in tow, and the Adamah (Chicago) humidity immediately wraps its wet arms around him threatening to place its hand over his nose, denying him air. He draws in a labored breath and begins walking toward the overpass, knowing that the homeless and drug addicts will be clamoring for coveted dry spots for the night. His blonde hair weighed down by the rain cascades over the shoulders of his drab, olive-green Army jacket as he continues on, his head down to avoid the raindrops on his face. He despises Amy for her brutality, but Charlie likes the recruiters to go out in pairs for safety, it's ironic but true. Charlie would end the life of a groupling out of boredom but wanted them to travel in pairs.

In Amy's other life, when she was human, she was a highly successful dominatrix with a well-hidden heroin addiction, living in her glass tower high above the city. Powerful, rich men got their jollies off being bossed and whipped by a petite, wholesome-looking girl and they paid big money for the humiliation. Her previous life is a prelude to her new career and she is one of Charlie's most sadistic recruiters. She entices both men and women with her sex appeal but takes pleasure torturing and humiliating them. She is a short ginger, about five-foot-two with green/blue eyes and plump breasts that served her well in both lives.

The rain creates an optical illusion of a mosquito net over the street lights, or possibly a fairy sprinkling her dust cocooning the eerie yellow light underneath. As the two recruiters pass a row of abandoned buildings, their shadows play hide-and-seek, their silent stalkers closely tracking them. In Adamah, Ryan and Amy have the flexibility to make decisions on their own and the freedom to act. As grouplings they are not able to comprehend their current dismal state and cannot remember their lives before they evolved, even in Adamah.

If Ryan was able to recall his last day before becoming a groupling, he would remember the fun he was having; he met up with his friends Joey, Lance, and Jeremy at their makeshift fort, the 'cabana,' and smoked some weed that Joey stole from his older brother. Their plan that night was to go to a party, meet chicks, and stay out until the sun began to rise. On their way to the party, they got sidetracked by a Thriftway Building Center that was under construction. The teenage boys could not resist the temptation of an unsecured construction site. They found their way to the top of the roof and were pretending they were in Vietnam ambushing the Viet Cong, throwing rocks as grenades. One of them hit a car and they were about to be trapped on top of the building when Jeremy yelled out, "Every man for himself!" They all started running down the stairs.

They breached the back door of the Thriftway building, one of Charlie's portals, and collided into Charlie in the alternate world-Sheol, beginning their horrific summertime journey. Of the four boys, Ryan was the only one that did not have a specific purpose for Charlie. So, Charlie melted his brain, figuratively speaking, and forced Joey to murder him in front of the other boys. Charlie had some sort of voodoo magic mind control over Joey making him obey without thinking or questioning him.

Ryan and Amy continue their walk down the abandoned street in silence. They have only one thing on their mind: to recruit. The overpass was approximately a mile away from the drug den and they walked slowly, taking their time, allowing the eerie darkness to drape the city. They can hear the cars traveling overhead and Amy is perplexed the cars' occupants are oblivious to what is happening right under their noses. The grouplings target easy prey: the homeless, runaways, and drug-addicted. They can be manipulated with drugs or money and if they come up missing no one will notice or care.

Ryan was the exception; he was at the wrong place at the wrong time. Charlie kept him around to use as bait knowing the boys would eventually figure out that he is still alive. Charlie allowed Lance to *see* Ryan when he crossed the threshold each night, hoping it would not take Lance long to figure it out and come for him. After Charlie's plan to use Lance, Jeremy, and Joey to fuse the two worlds together failed, he's been trying to bait them back into Sheol so he can finish the job. When the boys escaped, they did not know that Ryan was a groupling. They thought Ryan was killed in Adamah and would not be able to come back. After they defeated Charlie, and Ryan was not with them, the kids assumed the worse.

———

Ryan and Amy are one block away from the overpass now and can hear the degenerates chattering among themselves like rats in a gutter. Amy shivers but not because she is cold. She shivers because they repulse her and she's trying to shake their imaginary stench off of her. Someone is playing a guitar and singing an out of tune version of "Hey Jude" at the back of the overpass and another has a battery-powered boom box playing Kenny Loggins' "Footloose." Both people are increasing their volume to try and drown out the cars overhead, but the music crescendos into an annoying, nonsensical melody that's harassing everyone within earshot.

Amy thinks to herself, *Soon there will be a fight.* She smiles. She always gets excited when she nears the overpass, close enough to taste them in the air. She knows she will soon find some unwilling lost soul and trick him or her into following her back to the den with the promise of sex or drugs. But Amy will need to satisfy her lust first.

Ryan will be patient until she does. He will not help her, but he will enable her by looking the other way. He brushes his soaked hair away from his eyes so his view is unobstructed, the overpass is packed tonight. *It will be easy pickings*, he thinks.

Ryan is in the lead now, walking in the gutter instead of the sidewalk. He likes the feel of the water as it soaks his feet through his Converse All Stars. It reminds him of something or sometime, but he can't quite place his finger on it. It doesn't matter. It's a simple pleasure and he enjoys it when he can. Ryan is preoccupied with his own thoughts and doesn't notice Amy turn into the alley and even if he did, he would not care. He knows what she's going to do and he wants no part of it. He kills for Charlie, but he has no choice. His free will is suppressed and it provides him no enjoyment. He would not do it if given the option. He trudges ahead, enjoying the rain until he reaches the overpass. The first thing he is going to do is find the guitar player and smash her guitar.

———

Just short of the overpass, Amy pauses as Ryan continues. She is at the entrance of the pitch-black alley affording herself a few moments to observe her prey. Satisfied, she begins prowling along the wall for concealment, her plump red lips formed into a conniving evil grin. The couple inside continues with their debauchery, oblivious to their new friend. They can't see her, but she can see them, one on both knees and the other has his back pressed against the wet brick wall, both hands on his amour's head. She is feet away from them now and can smell the sex in the air, bewildered that they still do not notice her. The groans from the big man remind her of something that she can't quite place, but it burns in the pit of her stomach. If someone could flip the memory switch ON, she would remember the youth minister of her church group and how he led her behind the bushes of their summer camp cabin to play hide-and-seek. He had a mustache that itched against her skin and he smelled oily like a big, hairy green olive.

"Excuse me, gentlemen, but do you know where I can find my pussy—cat?" Wordsmithing in her best damsel-in-distress voice, she is now standing directly in front of the two men, legs spread, and her hands on her hips, her black high heels adding at least three inches to her height.

The big man against the wall opens his eyes in shock. His jeans are gathered down around his ankles and his wrinkled, blue, security-guard shirt pulled up above his big gut.

"What the fuck, shit," he blurts with fear in his voice. When he sees Amy, his attitude completely changes and he smirks. He thinks he's safe. No cops. Just a teeny-tiny little girl. "What ya' want little girl? Next?"

His hands are still holding his partner's head down. His partner giggles against the man's meaty, hairy thigh.

Amy moves closer and places her hands gently on top of his and says, "Yes please."

The man's shit-eating grin grows larger and Amy can see his yellow-stained teeth in the darkness and it angers her. *No respectable person would allow their teeth to rot like that*, she thinks.

The man's partner tries to turn his head to look up at her, tries to get up off his knees. The touch from Amy's petite hands immobilizes both of them like a blast from a freeze ray gun. She likes her victims this way and now she is going to have her fun.

"Okay, but it's going to cost you a cigarette," she says, kicking at a puddle, splashing water on the smaller man's backside.

"Hey, knock that shit off or I'm gonna bitch slap you," he says, still unable to move.

"Oh. I don't think you're going to do anything but suck that nasty, hairy *johnson* until I tell you otherwise," Amy says, turning the young man's head back into position to service the big man.

"Why can't we fuckin' move, TJ?" the younger one asks with fear in his voice.

The big man, TJ, begins to realize something isn't right, and he finds himself in a position he's not used to. He's scared.

"This bitch is some kind of witch." TJ's voice is now cracking from fear. "We're sorry lady; let us go please. I have a wife and daughter, and Darrel's a Jew."

Amy thinks, *That makes no fucking sense,* and then laughs out loud and starts singing:

All your life you've never seen
A woman taken by the wind
Would you stay if she promised you heaven?
Will you ever win?
Will you ever win?

She summons her power and flicks her right hand backward and Darrel's body awkwardly flies through the air, crashing hard against the wall behind them. TJ can't believe what he just saw and begins screaming. Amy gives him a school-teacher glare and gestures across her lips as if to zip them closed. TJ instantly shuts up. Unable to open his mouth, unable to talk. Invisible hands sew his lips together and he can feel every needle prick and the thread heat up as it's pulled taunt. He can only whimper through his blood-soaked lips. She looks like a little old lady trying to push a refrigerator as she gestures with both hands and TJ slams back into the wall—immobilized.

Although he can't speak, he can cry, and seeing the grown man's tears mix with the rain and run down TJ's face only heightens Amy's anger-lust. She feeds off fear, off the pain. She marches over and picks Darrel up by grabbing a handful of hair so he is again on his knees. She cut her eyes over her shoulder to make sure TJ is watching and with one hand hooks his upper jaw (maxilla) and the other below (mandible) and rips Darrel's jaw apart with ease. His lower jaw hangs exaggeratedly low, connected only by the ripped skin near his ears. The skin is the only thing keeping his chin from resting on his chest. Ignoring his pitiful gurgles, she grabs Darrel by his hair again, his knees hovering above the ground and walks her dog over to TJ. TJ's puffy, red eyes plead for mercy. He will not receive any tonight. Amy is not in a giving mood. When they are close enough and TJ can see the carnage of Darrel's face, his breathing grows frantic and he tries to scream, tries to plead, but he can do neither.

Amy positions Darrel so both of the men are postured as she found them just minutes ago. Like a ventriloquist, she throws her voice while working Darrel's mutilated mouth, "Do you like the color of my lipstick, big boy?"

Darrel passed out from the pain.

Earlier in the night, in his stupid apartment, TJ buttoned his stupid uniform, disgusted that he was only a security guard when he knew deep down he should be a cop. If it wasn't for his wife, early in their marriage when they were starry-eyed kids, calling the police and accusing him of choking her, and the visible bruising around her eyes and neck, he would be. He was raised abusive, watching his dad blame his mom for all of their problems and taking it out on her. To him beating your wife was part of a normal relationship. So sometimes he drinks a little too much or does a little too much coke or meth and takes it out on her because she deserves it. Tonight was one of those nights for him and on his way to work he stopped at his 'make me feel better about my miserable life' spot. He haggled a price for a quick blow job with Darrel, a street whore, who TJ knows he can get a little rough with and let off some steam from both his heads.

"Big boy, can I suck your cock?" Amy asks in her best sexy male voice. No answer. "Oh playing hard to get huh. Okay I'll do it for…a cigarette." She starts laughing at herself.

TJ is mortified but unable to do anything. What happens next is his worst nightmare. Actually, it's every man's worst nightmare and TJ doesn't have to be a rocket scientist to know what's going on. Amy tugs TJ's limp dick so it's positioned in front of Darrel's disfigured mouth and slams Darrel's lower jaw upward, shattering his teeth and TJ's jagged dick separates from his body. TJ's eyes just about burst out of his head and his whimpers are so loud that they sound like full throttle screams. Darrel is brought out of unconsciousness from the new acute pain and like TJ is muted by the magic thread that sewed their lips together. She releases both of them and they collapse onto the ground wiggling and squirming like earthworms drawn out of the dirt by the rain.

While Amy was playing with her boys, Ryan found his guitar hero and sauntered up to her with his best solo Lambada moves shuffling his feet. He sits next to her on the curb and pretends to be enjoying her performance by swaying to her music with a big smile on his face, eyes closed. She ends her song and Ryan enthusiastically claps and says, "Encore, encore that was great."

At the same time, he's thinking, *You fucking shittin' me. I'm going to bust that out-of-tune, piece-of-shit guitar.*

"Thank you, stranger. Did ya really like it? I mean I only been playin' for a couple of years. I teached myself. Are ya from around here? I never see ya before. Where's your bag? Ya have a tent or just a—?"

Ryan holds up a hand still smiling, still pretending.

"Wow, you talk a lot. You smoke a little crack?" He raises that same hand to his lips to mimic smoking a joint. "When was your last hit?"

"How ya know?" she asks, trying to sound innocent. "Is it that readable?" Strumming the strings on her guitar, she's looking down, more embarrassed than anything. She perks up and glances at Ryan. "Why? Ya got some? Do ya? I only need a lil bit. I'll play ya another song." Her eyes dart back down. "Or I can do somethin' else if ya want, anything. Just tell me."

Ryan is repulsed but doesn't show it. The girl's clothes are filthy and he can smell her from where she is sitting and it's not good. Her face is pocked from constantly picking at it and she is missing her right lateral incisor, long ago rotted away. She has a crew cut, but Ryan can tell it's greasy and filthy.

She catches Ryan looking at her hair and says, "I had to cut it on account I got lice. It was long and beautiful before." Pretending to flick her long hair back with her hands, she giggles. "So, do ya?"

"Do I what? Have some crack?" he asks as he leans back and pulls a small paper kite out of his front pocket. When the girl sees the folded paper, her eyes light up and she starts fidgeting.

"Give me, give me, please," she pleads with her voice and eyes. "I'll do anything. Want to have a fuck? I'm horny. Let's smoke some of that." She points to Ryan's hand. "Then we can do whatever you want."

She's now standing in front of Ryan, swaying her hips trying her best to look sexy.

Ryan pulls a small, glass pipe out of his jacket pocket. It's a crack pipe with a little stem and a round bowl with a hole at the top. The bottom is black from the lighter and burnt impurities and there is a white residue trailing up to the tip. The girl gets really excited and sits down close to Ryan. Too close for comfort. Ryan slides over slightly but not enough to be noticed. He opens the kite and empties the contents into the pipe. It's a small amount, maybe enough for two hits. He plans it that way. He has just enough to show his recruits that he has drugs so they will follow him back to the den.

"Here. Hit this. I think you'll like it," he says, holding it up to her lips and flicks the Bic lighter for her. Her eyes get large as she watches the smoke build and swirl around inside the glass and then she heartily inhales and drops onto her back. She refuses to exhale, relishing the toxic concoction in her lungs, and suddenly she sits up straight and blows what little smoke is left out of her mouth.

"Damn dog, that's sum good shit." Her brown eyes have instantly dilated. Charlie keeps his grouplings supply of drugs constant and the purity the best in all of Chicago. "Ya got more? Pleeze gimme more. I know ya got sum." She reaches over, feeling Ryan's pockets.

"Yeah, I got more, all you can smoke…or shoot," he says looking down at her arm. "You gotta come back to my place. What do you say?" He's leaning into her, bumping her shoulder with his.

Holding her guitar by the neck, she jumps up from the curb and says, "Can I bring my guitar? I'll play for you all night."

Ryan stands and stretches, listening for raindrops but unable to hear anything over the cars and the boom box. "Yeah, let's go." He thinks, *I'm going to wreck that fucking guitar*. A microexpression of disgust flashes across his face, too fast and subtle for the girl to notice.

Satisfied, Amy takes a second to admire her work. Both men lie on the wet ground, the rainwater diluting her life-size bloody canvas. To put them out of their misery, she rams the blade of her

Benchmade knife into each of their ears, pushing upward into the brain, ceasing all electrical current. They are both dead and they will never be grouplings. She killed them in Adamah.

Before she leaves the alley to locate Ryan, she decides to have some fun with whoever finds them. She's in the mood to play hide-and-seek. She tears Darrel's jaw the rest of the way off. When she pulls, the flesh rips down the neck to the collar bone exposing the larynx. She didn't plan it that way, but to her it was a bonus. She summons her strength and flicks her hands upward and TJ's body flies through the air, finally resting on the guardrail of the fire escape at the top of the building. His body drooped over at the waist, his pants still down at his ankles, he'll be mooning whoever finds him. She looks around the alley and spots a dumpster that will be perfect for staging Darrel. She places his body between a wall and the big green receptacle and slides it back, pinning him in an upright position, resting his upper jaw on the filthy edge. Whoever finds him will have no idea until they move the dumpster. She giggles to herself proudly. Clutching TJ's dick and Darrel's jaw, she walks out of the alley and stages her final piece. She centers the lower jaw with its demented version of Billy Bob teeth at the entrance right before the sidewalk and places the severed dick to look like a tongue sticking out, mocking the world. She feels wickedly proud of herself as she leaves. Her game took too long and Ryan is already on his way back to the den with his recruit so she has to hurry and catch up empty-handed. Someday Amy's luck is going to run out and someone will end her life in Adamah and she will be gone for good.

Ryan leads the guitar-playing junkie up to the back door of the den and pauses, glad that the small talk on the way over is done. Every night when he reaches the threshold, he gets an unusual feeling in his head that should mean something important but doesn't. For a nanosecond, Ryan's brain recalls his life before becoming a groupling. It's a flash and he doesn't actually visualize anything; it's more of an emotion and then it's gone and Charlie's hold on him reaffirms itself. It's like a missing puzzle piece that is needed to bring the rest of the puzzle into context so it can be finished.

Ryan doesn't know it, but Lance receives a vision of him crossing the threshold each time. It's only a small shard of a kaleidoscope of fragmented dreams, but Lance knows he's alive. The visions have been more frequent and vivid lately and Lance is even getting them while wide awake.

Ryan opens the door at the same time Amy catches up to them. They acknowledge each other with a nod but don't speak a word.

The guitar player notices the blood on Amy's clothes but does not say anything. The only thought running through her head is how good the next fix will feel.

It's pitch black inside and Ryan grabs his recruit's hand so he can lead her through the maze. They go up to the second floor. She's bumping and tripping like all the others before her. They arrive at a mattress pushed up against the corner of the walls. Ryan helps her sit and tries to take her guitar out of her hand.

"Yo whatcha doin? That's mine," she says in the darkness, unable to see who's pulling at her guitar. She feels different being here. It's scary, dark, and smells, and she has a bad feeling, but her urge to get her next fix trumps her common sense and need for safety.

"It's me, Ryan. I'm just setting your guitar over here so it doesn't get broken." He flings it across the room. It lets out a blunt *twang* as it hits the floor. Before she can object or ask why he threw her guitar, he says, "You never told me your name, sweetheart."

"Everyone just calls me Cat. Did you throw my guitar?"

"Of course not," he says, as he produces a syringe seemingly from thin air. It has a fatal dose of heroin. "You want to get high? I got a healthy bump right here."

Cat's eyes have adjusted to the dark and she can faintly see Ryan standing in front of her holding the syringe. Her heart begins beating rapidly and she can taste the drug in her mouth and a feeling of euphoria comes over her even before she rides the lightning. For the first time, Cat realizes how handsome Ryan looks with his blonde hair and slender body. It could be the promise of the drugs or maybe her mind is trying to convince her he's cute since she did promise him sex. She doesn't know and right now she doesn't care. All of the noise around her begins to fade as she concentrates on the needle, oblivious to the moans, and intermittent barks of pain as other grouplings turn their prey.

"Fuck ya, let's do it! But hit me in my feet my arms are pretty flat," she says, holding her left foot up for Ryan.

Ryan can see the track marks in between her fluorescent green toenails and kneels down thinking that at least this way she won't suffer long. Ryan prefers to give fatal doses of heroin to his recruits to minimize their pain and suffering. He cannot control much of his new life but he can control this.

The other grouplings prefer to make their recruits suffer as they are converted, and they kill them slowly, brutally. Ryan injects Cat and pushes the plunger deep, watching the emotion in her eyes go from pleasure to registered horror, realizing she just shook hands with the Grim Reaper.

Cat nods out on the mattress and her breathing becomes shallow, a death rattle, as she steps out of her body and into her new role as a groupling. Ryan patiently waits for the last of her life to leave and lifts her hand to make sure. Her lips and fingernails turn blue from the lack of oxygen. Her life expires in pathetic fashion with drool and vomit covering her face and adding to the eclectic fluids already soaked into the mattress. When she rises, she will have crossed over and will begin her new life, a slave to Charlie.

———

Most mornings Lance wakes up in a cold sweat more tired than when he went to bed. So far his summer vacation has not gone as planned. Since the night he, Jeremy, and Joey survived their run-in with Charlie, nothing has been the same. That's especially true with Ryan missing. Lance tries to remember his dreams from the night before and recently he has been writing what he remembers down as soon as he wakes. Lance never remembers much, but each morning he wakes with a feeling that Ryan is still alive somehow, somewhere. His notes are sparse. They're usually one or two scrawled words, rarely a full sentence, but one common theme is the word: Ryan. Lance doesn't even know if Ryan's name comes up because he's actually dreamed about Ryan or if he only wishes he did. Lance has not confided in anyone about his dreams. Who would believe him? He hasn't even told Jeremy or Joey. In fact, he has not talked to either of them since the morning they woke up in Jeremy's room after their journey to Sheol. It's all too crazy and their adolescent brains cannot comprehend or refuse to understand what happened, but, it's all true.

Soon Emma, the guardian angel that aided Lance in his defeat of Charlie, will tell him that his dreams are actually visions of Ryan crossing over thresholds and that he is alive.

CHAPTER 2

EXTRA! EXTRA! READ ALL ABOUT IT!

For about a week after the incident, Lance has moped around his trailer house. His mom keeps asking if anyone has any new news about Ryan and also bugging him to go outside and get some sun. He knows he should, but he can't bring himself to leave the safety and comfort of his home. He's been spending his days on the sofa being a couch potato or in his room listening to cassette tapes of Led Zeppelin, The Doors, Eagles, and Mötley Crüe. In the last week, he's showered zero times and brushed his teeth twice. Hell, he hasn't even changed out of his pajamas: a pair of red shorts and a plain V-neck T-shirt.

Ryan keeps swimming in and out of Lance's thoughts and Lance can't shake it. He knows Ryan is alive and, if it's true, then they need to find him. But how can Lance know for sure? They watched Joey murder him. But was it in Adamah or Sheol? If it was in Sheol he can still be alive. What evidence does he have besides his notebook by his bed? Where would they even begin to look? He's confused and depressed.

Jeremy is in the same emotional state as Lance and pretty much mimicking what Lance has been doing: nothing. Jeremy's big brother can't get a rise out of him. He even tried to coax him into a fight, hoping to get some type of emotional reaction; he didn't take the bait. His brother does not know what's wrong with him, but he knows that Jeremy is not himself. He believes Jeremy is acting like someone that's been traumatized by something, but he knows that can't be true. Usually, Jeremy tells Brian everything significant that happens to him. But this is one secret he is keeping to himself. His big brother has no idea about his suicide in Sheol, or that his blood is one of the links needed by an evil demon to merge two worlds.

Joey, on the other hand, has been living life to the fullest. He's been swimming at Veteran's Park, boogie boarding in the canal, and spending a lot of time with Larry and his buddies. His excuse for hanging out with Larry is Lance and Jeremy refuse to leave their homes; it's a valid excuse. Joey has compartmentalized what little he remembers about his experience in Sheol. Plus, he's just cut from a different cloth than the other two.

Lance's mom hasn't noticed his fragile emotional state now that she has a new boyfriend, Mr. Nobody. Nobody knows his name and nobody cares. He'll be gone in a month or two so why even learn what to call him?

Lance is lying on the couch with Bear at his feet watching re-runs of *Knight Rider* and waiting for *Three's Company* to come on. He has a crush on Suzanne Somers, but who doesn't? He suddenly has an epiphany, leaps to his feet, and races into his bedroom. Bear barks and follows closely behind, not sure what's going on. Lance grabs his notebook and frantically flips through the folded and ripped pages and suddenly...

"Aha!" His finger rests on *Emma*. A name, but what does it mean? It's the only time it has come up in his journal writing and he doesn't even remember why he wrote it down.

"Emma, Emma, Emma...hmm," he says out loud, looking at Bear while tapping his finger on the notebook and his foot on the floor. The name is familiar, but he can't quite place who or why he knows it. Maybe its someone from school?

"Big Bear, do you know Emma?" he asks, now tapping the top of Bear's head and rubbing his floppy ear. "You're no help, boy," he says, still caressing his head.

Bear looks up at Lance with the only look he knows: love and loyalty. Bear is a small, scraggly, wire-haired dog with big, floppy ears and an infinity for barking. Lance named him Bear because he wanted a dog as big as a bear to wrestle with when it got older. Even though Bear is not large in stature, in Lance's eyes he's a T-Rex.

Lance leans back and falls onto his unmade bed and settles with his head resting against the wall and his feet dangling off the side. Bear starts licking the bottom of his feet tickling him.

"Get up here, Big Bear. How are you gonna fight off predators if you're a teddy bear?" Bear jumps up and settles under the crook of Lance's knees. Lance lies there in his bed with the Eagles playing on his stereo, oblivious to the music, deep in thought. He wonders what Jeremy and Joey are doing right now and what the scribbling in his dream book means. He can't put his finger on something that he knows is important. It's just out of reach of his consciousness and who *is* Charlie?

After about an hour, Lance gets out of bed hungry and thirsty. He walks into the small kitchen to see what he can find for himself and Bear. He sidesteps the piece of ripped linoleum in the center of the kitchen and the thought of ripping it up pops back in his head, but today is not the day.

He hasn't had much of an appetite lately and it's good thing. There's not an abundance of food in the house. He hooks his toes under the refrigerator door and swings it open: milk, eggs, a pack of bologna, and some condiments. He grabs the bologna and sits on the couch, alternating between him and Bear. When the bologna is gone, he gets up to throw away the package and get a drink of water. As he walks by the tiny glass kitchen table that his mom bought earlier in the year at the Salvation Army, he notices a newspaper still rolled and secured by a rubber band.

He loves the rubber bands used on newspapers. They're always the heavy-duty kind that last. They make great weapons when he sets up his *Star Wars* figures and has battles in his room, although he hasn't done that in years.

He sits in one of the two chairs and starts stripping the rubber band off the newspaper. It's a local paper: the *Idaho Statesman*. Occasionally they deliver free papers to entice new subscribers. Lance knows his mom will never spend money for a newspaper unless it's close to Christmas and then she gets it for the coupons and sales ads. He flips through it searching for the comic strips. His favorite is *Beetle Bailey*. He stops mid-turn when his eye catches a headline:

BOISE BOY STILL MISSING

BOISE - Earlier this week, local authorities reported finding the remains of missing Boise, Idaho teenager Ryan Collins, in a shallow grave in the Oregon high desert approximately 50 miles from the Oregon-Idaho border. It was reported that the teenager had been abducted in Boise, possibly by an unknown number of adults traveling through the area in a 1970s blue-and-white Volkswagen minibus.

The police reported that the group might be part of a band of vagrants with devil-worshipping ties to a church in Southern California.

At the time of the discovery, police reported with "high certainty" that the mutilated remains were indeed the missing seventh-grader from Hillside Junior High School.

Today, authorities are backtracking on their previous claim after a dental exam of the deceased failed to match Collins's dental records. The body has not been identified at this time, and authorities are actively investigating.

Authorities are convinced Collins is still missing, and his case will be reclassified from a homicide to a missing person.

A request to interview Collins' family has been denied at this time.

Lance stops reading. Actually, he stops the moment after he sees Ryan's name in print. He knows this means Ryan can still be alive.

I'm right!

Now he needs to try and figure out how to prove it and then find him. He grabs Bear and gives his furry friend a big hug. Bear's tongue immediately goes into overdrive, licking Lance's face and ears.

"Okay boy, I know. I know we're both happy, but how are we going to find Ryan?" With both hands cradling Bear's head, the dog's tongue was lapping at air trying to coat Lance's face with slobber, but Lance stays just out of reach. Lance stands and begins pacing between the kitchen and the living room, deep in thought, and talking to Bear out loud.

"How can we prove he's still alive? How do we find him?" He pauses. "Who is going to help us, Bear?" Still feverishly pacing, his mind churns overtime. "I need to settle down. I need to sit." He flops on the couch and Bear leaps up into his lap. "I can call Jeremy. But he'll think I'm crazy."

There's a knock on Lance's door.

———

Emma has been watching Lance since his return from Sheol, remaining just out of reach of his consciousness. She's been worried about his physical and mental state since the journey to Sheol. The horror Lance and his friends endured would place most sane men in an asylum. She's allowed him time to rest and regain his energy, but now she knows she must reveal herself and explain why Lance keeps having his nagging dreams about Ryan. And, she knows that Charlie is now actively searching for the boys. He was not destroyed like the kids believed when they left Sheol.

Lance leaps to the door and wildly pulls it open, expecting to see Jeremy on the other side. Instead, he sees a beautiful barefoot goddess of a woman, wearing a white lace dress. She has long, braided black hair, a 1960s or 1970s throwback flower-girl look.

"Emma!?" he says, perplexed that he knows her name. He instinctively blocks the door with his foot to keep Bear from running out, but Bear is obediently sitting on the couch, quietly staring at them both.

"Do you remember me?" she asks, waiting to be invited inside.

"I don't know, but your name is Emma, right?" He opens the door wider so she can step in. He motions for her to sit on the beat-up brown couch, half expecting her to decline so she doesn't get her dress dirty. Emma sits and Bear crawls over to her and lies against her right thigh. She strokes Bear's head and asks him to give her some privacy. Bear stretches and hops down off the couch and walks back toward Lance's room.

"I'm right, right? Your name is Emma?" Lance asks as he sits on the opposite end of the couch.

"Yes, Lance you're right. Do you know why I'm here?" She straightens her dress briefly breaking eye contact with him. "Do you remember anything about us?"

"Wait!" Lance jumps up and runs to his room sliding on the carpet. He returns a few seconds later holding his tattered notebook. His finger pointing to her name. This time he sits closer to

Emma so she can see the notebook. "I wrote your name down from my dreams. I've dreamed about you, right?"

"Lance, you and I have been more than a dream. We've been on a heck of a journey in Sheol. I didn't know how much you would remember. It appears not much." Emma shifts and crosses her legs at the ankles. "Do you remember when we first met? You were about nine years old. We did what's called '*glimpsing.*' We take you from your conscious state in Adamah and your mind travels to Sheol. People usually don't remember the experience or they believe it was a dream. It's different than physically entering into Sheol through what you call a threshold or a portal."

"No, it doesn't ring a bell."

"Do you know why you keep dreaming about Ryan?" she asks, mapping Lance's face looking for emotion, for a flicker or some signal that he comprehends. Instead, she sees sadness. His emotions for Ryan are strong and Emma knows she will need to be delicate, but they are running out of time. Emma reaches up and removes a silver chain necklace from around her neck. She holds it in her hand and displays it like a saleswoman at a fine jewelry store. "Do you remember this rock?"

She is again peering into his brown eyes. Clasped to the chain necklace is a silver dollar-sized flat rock, a talisman. The edges are rounded and there is a noticeable groove through the center. The rock is gray, but it looks like it was pulled out of a campfire with noticeable black striations. Lance shakes his head to indicate he does not know what it is or what it means. Emma leans into Lance, adjusting herself on the couch and places the necklace over his head. Like jolts of lightning, images and emotions flood Lance's mind. So much, so fast, he thinks he's going to get sick and pass out. The visions cause Lance to have a cataplectic attack and he collapses back into the couch.

The talisman is the same one that Lance carried on his previous journey into Sheol and the same one that saved humanity from Charlie's plan to merge the two worlds, which would have assured Erebus's rule. Emma is taking Lance *glimpsing*, but this time Lance is having an out-of-body experience, soaring high above each phase that happened during his previous trip. He's watching a cognitive replay of what happened to him and his friends the last time Charlie captured them.

Phase one: Lance, Jeremy, Joey, and Ryan are standing outside of the Thriftway Building Center after running out of the building trying to escape the big cowboy coming after them for throwing a rock through his windshield. Instead of the cowboy in their world, they meet the oddly dressed man in Sheol; they would later call him Charlie. They didn't know it then, but Charlie opened a portal at the back door of the Thriftway connecting Adamah and Sheol. Watching a replay of Joey murdering Ryan for the second time does nothing to blunt the emotion and fear Lance felt then and feels now. Lance knows it was Charlie controlling Joey, pulling Joey's strings like a puppet master. The large black vultures, Charlie calls highwaymen, carry Ryan's body off high above the clouds. They fly so close to Lance that he instinctively tries to move out of the way.

Phase two: They are driving through Sheol's barren red landscape in a beat-up Camaro without Ryan. They stop at a rundown gas station/diner and Lance is watching himself and his buddies making out with three very pretty girls inside the diner. Charlie is sitting on a stool observing them like a pervert at a peep show. Charlie becomes restless and the whole place breaks into pandemonium. The girls mutate into grouplings and Lance watches with newfound horror as they begin rotting. All three boys, Lance, Jeremy, and Joey, try to escape, but the doors are locked. Lance hands Jeremy the stone (the one around his neck now) and they both begin to calm down. They leave the diner and are back on the road, and the red Camaro is the only object moving in the unambiguous landscape. Lance is now viewing the back seat and watches as he hands Jeremy the talisman to try and settle him down after their horrific experience with the girls. Jeremy is not mentally strong enough or feels so hopeless that he believes his only option to free himself from this nightmare is to commit suicide. The Camaro is moving at more than one hundred miles an hour and Jeremy shoves Joey's driver seat forward and leaps out of the car head first. Lance is hovering high above the ground as he watches all of them run toward Jeremy's body in the street, and again the highwaymen swoop in to take the body into the orange sky to later deliver a groupling.

Phase three: The car finally rolls to a stop outside of the abandoned factory in the red dirt next to a dilapidated retaining wall. The ground is lurching and kicking like a violent roller coaster ride. Enormous chunks of the earth are swallowed away leaving black holes scattered across the landscape. Thousands of people from all directions are walking across the barren landscape toward the factory. Lance can see they are Charlie's grouplings. The sky is filled with highwaymen and Lance is swerving through the air to keep from colliding into them. He doesn't have to he's glimpsing; they pass through him like he's a ghost. They are inside the dark, smelly factory now, in a room made of gray brick and stone. Lance has been here before and remembers it's where he first met Emma when he was nine years old and she took him glimpsing. It's the first time Emma made herself known to Lance. He's hovering next to what once was Charlie's body, but is now an evil contorted mass spinning above the room.

Emma wants to emphasize what happens next so she slows the replay, Lance needs to understand that it was his bravery and courage that saved everyone.

Lance thrusts the talisman toward the portal forming in the center of the room. Demons are soaring out of the abyss at breakneck speed, their demonic screams add to the chaos already in the room. The talisman lands short and Lance lunges at the same time as Charlie descends from the endless ceiling. Charlie crashes into Lance with his gnarly, mangled talons digging deep into Lance's back. He's trying to get a good bite so he can lift Lance away. The phoenixes are circling and one of them dive bombs and crashes into Charlie exploding on impact.

Lance watches his former self, frozen in the prone position, his hand inches from the rock. He tries to project his movements to himself and force the Lance on the ground to push the rock forward; of course, he can't. And then it happens: Lance musters the strength and courage to overcome his fears, but before he can close the portal Charlie, wounded but not destroyed, re-emerges from the ceiling and knowing he has no more time, Lance forces the talisman into the portal closing it forever. Or so he thought.

Lance is jolted back to reality and finds himself lying on the floor in his trailer. Emma kneels beside him, rubbing his arm, soothing him. Bear is standing above his head, tail wagging nervously, letting out concerned little yips. At first, Lance can't move or maybe doesn't want to move. He's disoriented and the rush of horrible memories flood his brain causing a temporary short circuit of his senses. He eventually sits up and rests his back against the couch. Bear hops up and begins licking his ear.

"Knock it off, boy. I'm okay," he says, rubbing his eyes. His muscles feel like fragile rubber bands that could snap at any time. He tries to stand, but Emma gently pushes him back down. She sits next to him on the floor and wraps her arm around his shoulder and hugs him.

"Don't move, Lance. You've just had quite an experience. You need to gain your strength," she's still rubbing his shoulder.

Lance begins to collect himself and his muscles start to relax. Holding the talisman up in his hand he says, "Is this the rock, Emma? The one that I carried during my journey that sealed the portal?"

"Yes, it is."

"How am I remembering all of this now? I'm so confused."

"Lance, there's something we need to—"

"Wait! Wait! If Ryan was taken by the highwaymen the same way Jeremy was, that means he can still be alive, right!? That's why I've been dreaming about him. The dreams," he gives himself a mental high-five, feeling vindicated.

"Those feelings are actually visions of Ryan when he crosses a threshold between Adamah and Sheol. This world and the other."

"So, if Ryan is in our world right now, Adamah, why hasn't he come home?"

"He can't, Lance. Charlie's hold on his mind is too strong. He only allows Ryan to cross over because he knows you can see him. He wants to bait you back to Sheol to finish the job he started and you ended. The talisman did not destroy the portal that can merge the two worlds. Somehow it's open again."

"Then what can we do?" he asks in a small voice with no conviction. A forceful feeling of despair floods his mind causing his hands to shake uncontrollably. He wrings them together in a futile attempt to steady them.

"You're not going to like what I have to say. You need to go back to Sheol to save him," Emma says with a heavy heart.

"You're coming with me, right? I'll go. I want to go. I want Ryan back. But you'll come with me, won't you Emma?" The thought crosses Lance's mind that Emma may choose not to go or may not be able to go even if she wants. He snatches that bad thought and crumples it up like a piece of paper and mentally throws it out of his mind. She has to go; he won't give her a choice. If the portal is opened and Charlie is back, he needs her.

"Like before, Lance. I will always be with you. I've never left you. Of course, I will go."

Relieved, he says, "Will it be like this? Like a real person?" He's now holding her hand.

"No, not like this. Like before. I will be with you when you need me. I will help guide you. Your powers are growing stronger and that's the only reason I can appear before you like I am doing now. You'll be fine. I have to go, Lance, but remember we're always together." Emma begins to fade and slowly dissolves into the air like a spritzer of mist, and then she's just gone.

Lance feels lonely and more confused than ever now.

What power? I don't feel any power. How do I get back to Sheol? I don't even know where to start. It's not fair she left me, he thinks. *Wait, I'll get Jeremy and maybe Joey.*

He stands up on shaky legs and walks into the kitchen and reaches for the yellow phone on the wall and pushes the numbers to dial Jeremy.

"Hello, Jacobson residence," Jeremy's older brother answers.

"Hi, Brian. Is Jeremy home?" Lance asks while mentally cursing and flipping the phone off in his head.

"Who's this?" Brian asks, but obviously knows it's Lance's voice on the other end.

"Lance. Is Jeremy there?" Lance asks, aggravated.

"Bitch, even if he was, I wouldn't let him talk to you, fag."

"Please, Brian, it's important."

"Bullshit. Nothing you've got to say can be important."

Lance can hear Jeremy in the background asking who's on the phone right before he hears the click. Brian hangs up. Lance sets the handset back on the receiver and picks it back up waiting for the dial tone. He dials again.

"Hello?" Jeremy says.

"Whew, Jeremy. It's Lance. Thank God your brother didn't answer again."

"What do you want?"

"I have some news to tell you about Ryan. I know he's alive and I have proof." Lance waits for Jeremy to process the information and after a few seconds decides he's not going to answer him back. "Well, did you hear what I just said?"

Still nothing from the other end of the line. Finally, Jeremy says, "Fuck dude. Yeah, I heard you. What do you want me to do about it?"

Lance kind of expected that response and was ready.

"Meet me at the cabana; that's all you have to do. I'll show you why I believe he's alive and then you can make a decision." He waits again, listening to the slight hum of the connection. "Fuck dude. Come on. Will you meet me?"

Jeremy wants nothing more than to crawl back into his bed and go back to sleep, but he knows from Lance's tone that he's serious and probably won't leave him alone until he agrees to meet.

"Okay, I'll be there in an hour or so, I haven't showered in days and I stink."

"Sweet, see you then. Oh, I'm calling Joey to meet us too. It's important that all of us be there."

Lance waits for a response that he knows won't come. "Okay, bye, see you in an hour," he says as he hangs up the receiver, relieved that he was able to make this happen.

Before he called, he gave himself a 50/50 chance and that was only because they are such good friends and Jeremy, like Lance, has had time to rest and reflect.

He calls Joey next and knows the conversation will be much different if Joey is even home to answer. Joey answers on the first ring. Lance can visualize Joey lying on his bed with his Walkman next to him, his shoes still on, and Joey staring up at the poster taped above his bed of Lita Ford in black leather with her butt cheeks showing, holding a red guitar. The conversation is short and Joey agrees to meet them at the cabana in an hour. Lance flops onto the couch exhausted and rests.

Bear runs ahead of Lance and into Diana's yard. Diana is Lance's neighbor and he has had a crush on her from the first time they met. He remembers her lying in a lawn chair in her white two-piece bikini. One of her speakers propped up outside her window playing KISS's, "Calling Dr. Love."

Today, she's sitting on the steps leading to her front door. Her blonde hair is draped over her face. Her arms are hugging her legs. When Bear reaches her, she grabs him and cradles him for support. She's clearly distraught and Lance can hear the hurt and anger in her voice.

"You love me, don't you, Bear? You're a good boy," she whimpers, still hugging him.

"What's up, Reno?" Lance asks when he finally catches up. He calls her by her last name or sometimes he'll call her Dee. He slides next to her on the step.

"Hey, Sir Lance-a-lot. Nothing. My mom is being a bitch. She wants me to go my dad's early for summer vacation and I don't want to go."

"Why not? Is he a dick? Or does your boyfriend not want you to go?" Lance asks, probing for information about her relationship status.

"I don't have a boyfriend right now. Keeping my options open. Bear, will you be my boyfriend?" She holds Bear's head. "What? You will! Thank you, Bear. I promise to always be faithful."

I will! I will! Lance thinks.

"I'm going over to the cabana to meet Jeremy and Joey. Want to go?" he asks, expecting her to decline. He immediately regrets his decision. She's going to think they are crazy when they start talking about Charlie and Sheol.

"Is Bear going? If he is, then yes." She kisses his nappy head and continues hugging him.

Bear must be in heaven, Lance thinks.

"Of course. Let's go," he says with his heart skipping a beat that she said yes.

"Okay, let me lock my door and grab my flip flops," she says, already standing. She looks stunning in her cutoff jean shorts and faded black KISS shirt. Even with her puffy red eyes, Reno is beautiful and Lance is smitten.

───

When Jeremy walks into the cabana, he is met by Lance, Reno, Joey, and Bear.

"A full house, huh?" he says as he kicks over a milk crate to sit on.

All of them are sitting in a circle and blankly staring at nothing. Reno doesn't know what's going on and the three boys don't know whether they should talk in front of her or not. Since Lance invited them, he decides he will break the ice.

"How you guys been doin'?" he asks, looking down the hall of the burned-out abandoned trailer house, feigning concern for where Bear has disappeared. He is now second-guessing his decision to call the other two boys. His stomach agrees and decides to stage a revolt to show how serious it is. Lance's stomach makes a very loud and verbal objection that is amplified in the empty trailer. His face turns beet red and, if possible, he would disappear. Jeremy and Joey uncharacteristically barely acknowledge the sound. Under different circumstances, they would not let him live it down. Reno pretends not to hear it in an effort to minimize Lance's embarrassment.

There's real tension in the room and Reno finally picks up on it and realizes it's not because of Lance's stomach.

"Should I be here? Do you boys have something serious to discuss? I can leave." She begins to stand.

"Hell no! I mean no. I think it's alright if your here. Right guys?" Lance says looking at Joey and then Jeremy with pleading eyes.

"Yeah, I'm good with it," Joey says and pries his tried and true knife out of his pocket. He starts flicking it into the trailer floor sticking the landing every time.

Lance directs his attention to Jeremy. "Well?"

Jeremy is staring at his feet, pretending to concentrate on the soot he is bulldozing into a small pile with his shoe.

"I don't know. It feels weird. She'll think we're all crazy." He's still not looking up and fidgeting on his crate. It's obvious Jeremy is not with them mentally. He's a shell of his old confident self. Even Lance and Joey don't know how damaged he really is yet.

"I think I should just go. I've got to do some laundry anyway." And this time Reno does stand.

"No! Guys, I think she can help us," Lance stands and pulls the newspaper article out of his back pocket. "Reno, sit down. We want you here, don't we?"

Both Jeremy and Joey nod their heads and continue with what they were doing.

"Look guys, I grabbed the article. Look, it proves Ryan is still alive," he says with authority and crinkles the paper for emphasis. Now both boys perk up and look at him, interested.

"What the fuck. Why are you saying that?" Jeremy asks as he snatches the article out of Lance's hand. Joey slides over next to him so they can both read it at the same time.

As they are reading, Lance is mumbling, "Huh…huh…see, it's true."

Reno's interest is piqued and she holds her hand out for the paper, which Joey promptly hands her. All three boys sit in silence as she reads and digests the article. When she looks up, she has an expression of shock on her face.

"Do you guys really think Ryan can still be alive? Maybe hurt or kidnapped somewhere?" she asks, her olive-shaped green eyes twinkling. She reaches into her back pocket and pulls a pack of Virginia Slims and takes one out and lights it, holding it like a 60s actress with the end of her fingertips.

"According to this article, it's not him. So he must still be in Oregon. We owe it to him to try and find him. What do you guys say?" Lance asks excitedly.

"What are we going to do? Hitchhike to Oregon?" Jeremy mumbles.

If the tension in the room was not already heavy enough, it would be with what Lance says next. First, he knows he has to be careful; he doesn't know how Jeremy will handle it. He might get so upset, he just gets up and leaves. Lance fears if that happens, he won't see him again until the first day of school. Second, Reno. She is coming into this situation blind and with no context. She might think they are all crazy. She might get up and leave and never talk to Lance again. He contemplates his choices; he can go all in and just say it, *or* he can table it and wait for another opportunity.

He decides time is of the essence. They need to start looking for Ryan now and if he doesn't say it, he might not get another chance with Jeremy.

"Sheol," Lance says. His stomach verbally objects again, but it's in the form of a rumble this time.

"Shit. Did you just say shit?" Reno asks quizzically.

Joey slips his orange headphones over his ears and his brown eyes turn dark. Black. He clicks play on his treasured Sony Walkman and says, "S-H-E-O-L. He said Sheol. It's the other world."

All three boys are now staring blankly at the floor, lost in their own worlds, lost in their own thoughts, lost in their own nightmares.

Lance begins narrating the three-phases from Emma's visit when she took him glimpsing, the whole time clutching the talisman around his neck. He can feel the power in the rock. It feels warm and soothing in his hand. Lance doesn't know what, if anything, the other two boys remember, but Joey *did* remember Sheol. However, Joey has been an anomaly throughout this whole thing. Lance finally finds the courage to look at Reno, starting low at her feet and working his way up to her eyes. She appears amused and bewildered at the same time.

"Is this all real? Or have you boys been smoking a little too much?"

Silence.

"It's real, all of it. I don't know if I can go through this again," Jeremy finally says as he begins to stand and move toward the door. Before hearing Lance's narration of their journey, all of this was just an amalgamation of bad dreams and emotions. He could not quite put his finger on it. Now he can, and it scares the hell out of him.

"Wait! I know where to find him. I know where a portal is," Lance blurts out as he glides himself in between Jeremy and the door.

Joey instinctively stands, anticipating an argument or maybe even a fight.

Jeremy has neither the mental or physical strength for either. "Lance, get out of my way, please. I'm leaving."

"No, don't you want to find Ryan?"

"Dude, I'm tired of all of this. I won't be any good to anyone anyways. Please move."

Lance can see the exhaustion in Jeremy's face. His eyes are sunken with dark rings and his body is drooped over like an old man. Lance feels sorry for him, but he is mad that Jeremy won't help them find Ryan. Lance is tired too and would like nothing more than to go back to his trailer and sleep. He can't force Jeremy to go, so he reluctantly moves over to allow Jeremy free passage to the door.

Jeremy sinks his head lower and under his breath says, "I'm sorry," as he steps out of the fort. Deep in his heart, he wants to help his friends and knows that they will need him, but mentally he doesn't have the strength. He thinks that maybe a nap will help him think clearly as he slowly walks home.

"Well, I'm here and I believe you. When do we leave?" Reno asks as she drops her cigarette between her feet and crushes it out on the already burnt floor.

"Joey, you in?" Lance asks as he sits back down on his crate.

"You bet. I'm down. When do we leave...? Wait, where are we going?"

"Baker City, Oregon," Lance says as he whistles for Bear. He's going to need support as he explains this to them. Bear comes running out of the bathroom and leaps onto Lance's lap bringing dirt and soot with him. At first, Lance begins to push Bear off him but then changes his mind. His pair of Rustlers blue jeans are already dirty so what does it matter.

"Baker City!" both Joey and Reno say at the same time.

"Where the hell is Baker City?" Joey asks.

"The portal to Sheol is in Baker City and that's where Ryan is. Sheol." Lance says.

"How do you know?" Joey quizzes him.

"Emma told me."

"Who's Emma?" Reno asks.

"It's hard to explain. She's like my guardian, my protector. We never would have made it out of Sheol the first time if it wasn't for her," Lance says looking down at Bear, visibly embarrassed he admitted he has a guardian angel. Now he's surer than ever that Reno will think they're all crazy.

"Okay, I believe you. How are we getting there? Hitchhiking or riding our bikes?" she asks, silently skeptical, but if it gets her out of here, she's willing to play along.

Shifting Bear in his lap, Lance says, "I don't know. Maybe gather enough money for us to take a Greyhound?"

Joey pulls his knife out of the floor and starts pacing, "Fuck that. Let's steal a car."

"Right, and you know how to hotwire a car I suppose," Lance states sarcastically out loud, but in his mind he wonders if Joey really does know how to steal a car; he's surprised them more than once.

Before Joey has a chance to answer, Reno says, "We don't need to know how to hotwire. I know where we can get a car."

"Where?" Lance asks.

"My sister. She lives about a half-mile from here. I can ask to spend the night at her house and I'll sneak the keys when they fall asleep."

Solving the most significant piece of the puzzle, they continue discussing the rest of the logistics for the next few minutes. They have a plan.

Reno will spend the night with her sister and at midnight she will sneak the keys to the car and they will drive to Baker City. Easy right? She will leave her sister a note explaining that they are only borrowing the car and will return it safe and sound. Reno is sure her sister will understand and not call the police when she wakes up. Joey is bringing his dad's vacation maps and has been voted the navigator. All of them will bring as much money as they can, which won't be much. With that, they leave the fort and will all meet at Reno's sister's house at midnight. Joey agrees to meet Lance at his trailer at 11:30 p.m., and they will walk together.

Lance can't help but feel a little disappointed that Jeremy won't be joining them. He expected more from his friend. They both survived the same horrors at Charlie's cruel hands the last time. But then again, Jeremy did commit suicide in Sheol so maybe he is more damaged than Lance knows. If you die in Sheol you can come back to life, but maybe each time you die in that wicked world you lose a little bit of your soul. A little bit of yourself.

As Lance walks to his trailer, he can't shake that nagging feeling that he was not totally honest with his friends. He purposely left out the location of the portal, an abandoned pig slaughterhouse. He knew that if he mentioned it, Joey would give him shit. Joey seems to think that every abandoned building was once used as a serial killer's lair. He still swears that about their fort, the cabana. Lance arrives at his trailer and opens the small gate to let Bear into the yard.

He mumbles under his breath, "Shit's about to get real."

CHAPTER 3

HOUSE OF HORRORS

Lance is shoveling through his closet looking for equipment he thinks they will need for their journey back into Sheol, Black Sabbath's "War Pigs," mood music blaring through cheap speakers balanced on his windowsill. His bed is littered with miscellaneous trip items that he will sort through later.

He can't stop thinking about Jeremy and he's getting upset. Screw it. He decides he's going to call him. He storms out of his little bedroom shaking the trailer on its foundation as he steamrolls toward the kitchen. He's mad and is going to give Jeremy a piece of his mind. He snatches the phone receiver from the wall and pounds Jeremy's phone number with his finger and waits.

As he's waiting for someone to pick up on the other end of the phone line, he stretches the cord so he can reach the piece of linoleum on the kitchen floor that is peeling up and begins tapping it with his bare foot knowing it will not magically glue itself back to the sub-floor.

"Hello?"

Lance knows the familiar voice on the other end is Jeremy.

"Hey, Ryan needs you. He needs all of us. Why won't you come with us to help find him?" Lance blurts out, now stomping the damn disobedient flooring.

"Dude, I don't think I'll be any help and I feel sick."

"What kind of sick?" Lance asks, wondering if somehow Jeremy picked up some disease in Sheol or if Jeremy's suicide is affecting his physical state here in the real world.

"I just don't feel like myself. I'm tired, can't eat, can't sleep. I have no energy."

"That's exactly how I feel but I'm *willing* myself to stay strong for Ryan. You can too. He needs us, all of us."

Jeremy is lying on his bed with his pillow over his face thinking that if he presses hard enough he can end all of this.

"Did you hear me?" Lance asks.

Jeremy grabs his pillow and flings it across his room onto the floor, knowing he won't be suffocating himself anytime soon. "I heard you, dick, and the answer is still NO."

Both boys hang the phone up on each other simultaneously, so they both think they hung up on the other one, but neither feels a sense of satisfaction.

Lance is convinced Jeremy will not change his mind so they will go without him. He also makes a mental note that he will not be the first one to come crawling back to repair their friendship.

Charlie feels weak from his battle against Lance and those damn sentinel phoenixes. They nearly destroyed him. Lucky for him they were not in Adamah and when the phoenixes dragged him into the portal Erebus was waiting to free him. Erebus was not pleased and Charlie has paid a high price for his massive failure.

In Sheol, death is not eternal and pain is very real, and Charlie is going to learn that very soon. Erebus sentenced Charlie to an ad hoc Sheol prison to punish him for his failed commission and to add salt to the wound the warden is a woman. Her name is Madame Delphine.

Charlie's status and stature have been stripped from him along with his powers so he will not get any preferential treatment.

Groggily, Charlie licks his dry and cracked lips and tries to open his eyes but can't. They are cemented together by sweat, tears, and rheum. He tries to raise his hand to brush the crust away, but feels an odd sensation; he's raising his arm but his hand is not touching his head. Charlie is confused and his temporary blindness exaggerates his confusion. If he could see, he would see his left arm lying on a wooden table about five feet away from him. He knows that there is a fire in the room; its flames twinkle and shocks of red flicker behind his eyelids. He can hear groans of pain around him and his nose smells rot and decay.

Maybe dead animals?

He is still trying to decipher his current situation. Then he hears a voice, a woman's voice.

Humpty Dumpty sat on a wall,
Humpty Dumpty had a great fall;
All of the king's horses and all of the king's men
Couldn't put Humpty together again.

"Ooo, la, la, good you're awake, Mr. Stratt," Delphine says. She is using Charlie's real name, Abel Stratt.

"Where am I? Why can't I move?"

"Oh, well, Mr. Stratt you are being punished by Erebus and they have asked me to kindly tend to you. You are in my home. Well, not my real home, but my house in Sheol. Oh dear, I see why you're confused. You can't see. Silly me, let me help you."

She walks over to the table and picks up Charlie's limp arm. When the highwaymen brought Charlie to her she sawed one arm off and was going to start on the other when he woke. Normally, she would make sure her prisoner is awake to experience the pain, but he is different and she doesn't get to keep him for eternity; Erebus made that perfectly clear.

Delphine is notorious for her torture techniques and her mansion is the house of horrors in Sheol if such a thing is possible, and right now she's toying with Charlie.

"Damn right, you'll help. What do you mean Erebus asked you to 'tend to me?'" Charlie is furious that this woman is condescending and he's helpless to do anything about it.

Delphine dips Charlie's severed arm in a wooden bucket full of putrid blood and body parts and he feels the sensation of the cold liquid as if his arm was still attached to his body.

"Here you go, Mr. Stratt. Try not to poke your eyes out. I'm going to do that later," Delphine mocks as she brushes his hand across his eyes denying him the satisfaction of acknowledging his authoritative statement or answering his question.

Charlie feverishly blinks as the goop begins separating and he can finally see. He begins soaking in his environment, making a calculated assessment of his surroundings. It's not good.

He is in a wooden room lit by torches placed in sconces approximately every four feet apart or so. There's a blood-stained torture rack with crimson-colored ropes stationed in front of him. It is currently empty. There's a Judas cradle in the left corner of the room with an unconscious nude female victim with her hands and feet bound by ropes hovering above a sharp wooden pyramid. Later she will be slowly lowered in a modified sitting position onto the device, ripping as her bodyweight works against her. There is an iron chair in front of Charlie with a miserable occupant currently strapped to it. The man is sitting on hundreds of iron spikes of different lengths piercing his back, arms, legs, and feet. He either passed out from the pain or is already dead. He would have to be or he would surely be screaming. There is also a sawing area to Charlie's right. He can see the ropes and leather straps secured to the ceiling meant to hold its victim upside down, legs spread. Leaning against the wall is a three-foot–two-man, rough-cut saw, and a bucket to catch the blood sitting next to it. There are two pillories against the other wall securing two very vocal male victims, pleading with Delphine to have mercy.

She walks over to the wooden bucket and starts swirling her hand around, searching for the perfect body part. She pulls a rotting severed hand out of the liquid and folds the fingers down to make a fist as she slowly walks over to the closest screamer.

"Open your goddamn mouth. I'm going to give you something to shut you up," she says calmly, but her eyes flicker with excitement. She shoves the rotting hand into his mouth so hard he has a new exaggerated *Joker* smile slowly spreading across his cheeks. Delphine has to exert extra energy to get the extremity all the way down her victim's throat. He can't scream anymore. The victim can only moan and gurgle as he battles for air. The hand was severed about six-inches above the wrist and the poor soul has it all the way down his throat.

It reminds Charlie of a bass he once saw as a child with another large fish sticking out of its mouth, nothing visible but the tail, both of them floating on the topwater. One dead from being eaten and the other from *your eyes are bigger than your stomach* syndrome.

She wipes her own hands on her apron that's tied snugly around her waist.

"Not hearing much out of you now. But don't worry, I heard you before," she says to the other man, her pupils the size of buttons transitioning from excited to incensed, sweat breaking on her brow, pasting her black bangs to her forehead. She picks up her custom handmade tool. It resembles a macabre speculum. The duck bill spreaders have small rows of gaffs on the end to grab and hold the flesh inside the mouth. In between the spreaders is a circular appendage with gaffs on the inside to catch and hold the tongue. She calls this torture device her 'quack, quack.'

Staring the man down, she pushes on his chin like it's a Pez dispenser and with a giggle whispers, "Open wide for your treat."

The man begins to violently thrash in his bondages, but it's to no avail. His teeth shatter as she forcefully shoves the quack, quack into his mouth, capturing the tongue on the first try. She slowly begins turning the ornate iron handle on the end of the sadistic tool; her victim's mouth is forced open until his jaw breaks and unhinges, his tongue grotesquely twisted and bleeding seemingly levitating within the wrecked orifice. The poor man can do nothing but grunt and moan, tears streaming down his face, his eyes bulging.

Charlie is a sadistic murderer, but even this is too grisly for him.

She slowly turns toward Charlie and says, "Mr. Stratt, consider yourself lucky. What I am going to do to you will hurt, but it will end."

Her smile turns into a frown to show her disappointment that Charlie will not spend eternity with her. "Erebus wants you to finish what you started, but you must be punished for your past failure. If you don't, or can't, this will be your future."

She sweeps her hand in front of her so Charlie can take in her torture room. "These poor souls are with me forever because they failed just like you. I play with them and they die, and I resurrect them and start over. It never ends." She sighs. "The lesson today is DO NOT fail or this is your fate."

Charlie knows she is serious, and Erebus will not give him another chance. They must believe he is the only one capable of capturing Lance and Jeremy and using their blood to merge the two worlds. If not, he would join these tortured souls forever. He is now more determined than ever to leave Delphine's house and finish his plan to use Ryan to bait the boys back to Sheol.

Charlie stands on his weak, shaky legs, determined to leave. "What happened to my arm?"

"Oh dear, Mr. Stratt, you can't leave until we have dinner, but first let me give you a tour of my home," Delphine says as she grabs Charlie's other hand so she can lead him around, still holding his severed appendage.

"This is obviously my naughty room. Anything else you want to see in here?"

"No."

She leads him to the back of the room and through a double door. It's dark and Charlie can smell feces, mold, and rot. The smell is overwhelming to Charlie and that says something. It doesn't seem to faze Delphine at all.

Instead of a room, it's a long hallway of rusty, iron holding cells that remind him of an old prison set too close to the sea. The cells are vacant of everything except chained miserable bodies. No bed, blanket, chair, or even a bucket to go to the bathroom; they piss and shit in a narrow gutter that runs the length of the cell and empties somewhere outside. This is also where they have to get their water if they're thirsty. They wait for the once a day flush and when all the piss and shit clears, they scoop their drinking water with their hands and drink. The prisoners are wearing heavy iron collars with spikes on the inside diameter that assure compliance with a hearty tug or two.

As they walk past the cells, Charlie notices that almost all of the prisoners are missing limbs—arms, legs, or both—and he can't help glancing at his own shoulder. He will learn all too soon that Delphine loves the taste of flesh.

"This is where my permanent residents stay. I think it's quite cozy, wouldn't you agree?" she asks, nodding her head, Charlie nods, mimicking her without thinking about it.

They reach the end of the hall and go down two majestic flights of stairs to the ground floor of the mansion. It's opulent with a stupendous crystal chandelier and plush furnishings placed perfectly within the grand room. In contrast to the top floor, this floor is clean, bright, and beautiful.

Next, they arrive in a very large kitchen that would rival any commercial kitchen and the elephant in the room is not an elephant at all. It's a very plump woman wearing a long coarse black-and-white dress and simple black boots. An apron sloppily hangs around her waist and the same iron collar Charlie saw on the other prisoners hangs around her neck. Her chain is long enough to reach any part of the kitchen and its secured to a heavy metal ring on the floor.

"Miss Rebecca, how long before the gumbo is ready?"

"Simmerin' now, Miss Del. It will be ready by the dinner bell."

Delphine tosses Charlie's arm onto one of the prep tables and says, "I'm in the mood for shrimp cocktail too."

Rebecca has made this before and understands what Delphine wants. "Fifteen minutes ma'am and I'll bring it to you."

"You are the best. Make sure the roux is nice and dark now."

"Of course ma'am, jus' the way you likin it."

Delphine leads Charlie through the kitchen to the dining room. Before Charlie passes through the door that the servants will be using later tonight, he turns to take one last look at the cook. He immediately wishes he did not. Rebecca, wielding a large butcher knife slams it down and severs Charlie's fingers. He swears he felt the blade decapitate his fingers from the rest of his hand.

When they arrive in the dining room, Charlie is surprised that they are not alone. Sitting at the far end of a decorated dining table is another man. He looks small in contrast to the table. The table is large enough to seat forty or fifty guests. As they walk closer, Charlie can see that the man is about double Charlie's size; he's a very large man. A large man also missing one of his arms.

"Mr. Garrington, I would like to introduce you to Mr. Stratt," Delphine says as she waves for Charlie to sit opposite of Mr. Garrington so they can stare at each other. Delphine takes the seat of honor at the head of the table.

What the hell is going on in this sick bitch's head? Charlie thinks.

As soon as Delphine's modest rear end touches the cushion, a server quickly snatches a silver tray from a table stationed next to her and rushes to Delphine.

The room is so large that Charlie did not even notice all the servants, posted at the ready, when he entered.

Delphine whispers something into the servant's ear and the woman hurries off into the kitchen and reappears with a very large shrimp cocktail and places it in front of Miss Del.

"Gentlemen, this is one of my favorite appetizers. Mr. Garrington, thank Mr. Stratt for his contribution." She gestures.

Charlie is in disbelief. He thought he saw, what he saw, in the kitchen, but didn't want to believe it. Charlie's mind is scrambled as he tries to make sense of what is happening.

Is this bitch a cannibal? There's no fucking way I'm going to eat human flesh, especially mine.

"No, no, no fucking way! No fucking way!" Charlie yells as he begins to rise out of his chair.

"Sit, Mr. Stratt. The only way you can leave this house is after you've finished your dinner…every bite, or, you can join Mr.

Garrington and stay for good. In fact, I'll even entertain making you two roommates." She beams.

"What do you want? You want me to eat my own fingers?" Charlie asks, staring at the glass full of thick red sauce and four fingers and one thumb clinging to the rim.

"Yes, of course, but I always get the thumb, it has the most meat," she says, plucking the thumb and licking the cocktail sauce off of it. "Don't worry, Miss Rebecca removes the nails and bones." And with that, she bites the thumb in two, chewing, smiling.

Charlie cringes and Mr. Garrington stares emotionless. Mr. Garrington has obviously lost his mind years ago from the mental and physical torture under Delphine's care.

Charlie is frantically looking around the room for support, first to the man across from him sitting stoically silent, and then the servants. He will get none from any of them. They do not look like they are registering what is happening, their blank stares match their emotion: empty.

"Dig in… Now."

Mr. Garrington quickly grabs Charlie's ring finger and pops the whole thing in his mouth chewing like a cow, teeth grinding and pulverizing the finger into small manageable bites. Charlie's head is about to explode. His mind is frantic and confused. He sits frozen. After an internal tug-of-war, he decides that if he does not play along, he will never get out. He makes a mental note that once he finishes his mission he will return and feed Delphine her own limbs while he, and all of her victims, watch.

He grabs a finger, grimaces, swallows it whole, and gags.

"Good. Now don't ruin your appetite. We have a special gumbo. Mr. Stratt, thank Mr. Garrington for his contribution of this blessed meal we are about to receive."

Nothing.

"Well,…He's waiting."

Charlie looks into the man's vacant eyes.

"Thank you, Mr. Garrington."

"Excellent, bring out the gumbo."

All of the servants leap into action. Two of them scurry into the kitchen and another hurries to the table to ready the bowls.

Rebecca appears at the doorway, smiling from ear-to-ear, holding a steaming pot of gumbo as she hands it off to a servant. The other servant follows with accoutrements and drinks. Delphine claps approval and greedily rubs her hands together.

Looking at Mr. Garrington, she says, "I hope you taste as good as you look. Your meat should be soft and melt in our mouths. Thank you."

"Yes ma'am."

Rebecca does not leave the doorway until after Delphine takes her first bite and nods her approval. Satisfied she's safe, she disappears back into the kitchen.

Charlie's first bite is another finger.

At least it's not mine, he thinks as he shovels spoon after spoon into his mouth trying not to taste.

He finishes his bowl and is about to ask Delphine to release him when Rebecca appears at the door.

"Miss Del, are you ready for the main dish?"

"Yes, of course, please bring it out."

Both men look at each other quizzically and Charlie suddenly gets sick to his stomach. He was mentally able to will himself to swallow his own finger and eat the man across from him, but he doesn't think he can take anymore.

A servant carts out a large silver platter with a cloche disguising the surprise underneath. The servant stops at Delphine and with a curtsy, removes the lid. Delphine giggles with excitement looking from Charlie to the man for approval. She gets none.

"Yes, yes, hurry, it looks delicious. Gentlemen, I get the tongue. You can each have an eyeball and then you must try some cheek," she says, pounding her fists on the table.

Staring up from the ornamental platter is a steaming, roasted female head complete with cloudy sunken eyeballs.

Delphine grabs an ear and it falls off. She yells, "Miss Rebecca, you've outdone yourself this time. The meat is so tender it just falls off."

Rebecca re-appears at the doorway proudly shaking her head in affirmation and curtsying back into the kitchen.

Delphine insists all three of them feast until there was nothing left but bone, teeth, and the green garnish surrounding the skull. Fat and happy, Delphine offers her guests dessert. They both politely decline. She gestures to the servants and they rush over to help Mr. Garrington out of his chair. As they pass her, she raises her hand and all three of them freeze. She yells for Rebecca who immediately appears in the doorway.

"Miss Rebecca, tomorrow night I would like to have rump roast for dinner," she says as she slaps Mr. Garrington's ass.

Rebecca replies, "Of cours' Miss Del, but not overcooked, jus' the way you like it."

Charlie steals a glance at Mr. Garrington's face and even though he has showed no outward emotion before, this time Charlie does see a micro-expression of fear, and thinks, *I knew it, I knew he could comprehend what the hell was going on, poor bastard. Waiting around to be slowly eaten alive.*

Delphine must now honor Erebus's command and release Charlie. She's mildly sad, she was having so much fun with him. She gestures toward the front door.

"Does this mean I'm done, Delphine?"

"Have you learned your lesson? Would you be willing to volunteer and stay a bit longer?"

"Am I free? That's all I want to know." His eyes are burning into her.

"Yes, Erebus has released you. You are free to go. I hope you enjoyed your brief stay and Mr. Stratt, you are welcome back anytime." Delphine shoots a wicked southern smile at Charlie as he rises from his chair.

"Show me the door, please."

"Of course." She stands and leads Charlie back through the grand room to the front door. Charlie opens the heavy door and does not feel the invisible restraints that were so prominent just seconds before, and he knows he's free. But just to be sure, he steps outside of the threshold and onto the marble steps leading to the street.

Turning back to face his hostess, he boldly says, "Oh, Delphine, trust me when I say this. When this is over, I'm going to return and you will be the main course." Satisfied, he begins to walk away.

"Mr. Stratt, I already know this, but like you, it will not be for eternity," she quips.

Bull-Fucking-Shit, it won't, he screams in his head.

Once this is over, or maybe sooner, Charlie is going to make sure she suffers and suffers forever. He is already playing out the conversation in his head between Erebus and him. He is going to insist that the reward he wants for merging Adamah and Sheol is her—Delphine. And he knows that if he can succeed, Erebus will be happy to give her to him.

Lance glances at the General Electric clock-radio renting space on a cardboard box next to his bed, and it reads 11:08 p.m. in red digits. He grabs his black Jansport backpack full of supplies and equipment that he thinks they may need for the journey and quietly slips out of his bedroom and finally the trailer. He doesn't want to wake his mom and he knows Joey will do something dumb like knock on the front door, setting off their alarm system: Bear. Once outside, he takes a big breath and inhales the refreshing summer air. Lance loves the smell of Boise. It has a distinct, clean, mountain smell mixed with a little bit of city fumes. The trailer park is dimly lit by street lamps and all of the streets are quiet with the exception of a few passing cars. He knows that Joey is probably at the cabana watching the minute hand on his flamboyant Swatch watch waiting for it to strike the six, indicating 11:30 p.m., before he heads to Lance's house.

"Bear, damn it! How did you get out?" Lance asks, watching his dog rumble toward him, ears flopping, tongue hanging out, and a smile on his face.

Bear catches up to Lance and keeps going. He knows that in this direction the next stop is at the boy's fort.

Oh well, I guess I'll bring him. I hope he behaves and doesn't get hurt, Lance thinks, glad, deep down, that Bear will be joining them. *Wait, how did he get out? I know I closed the door.*

Lance did not see Emma open the door after he left to let Bear out. Emma knows that Bear will be needed for the journey. She's sad. It's only a feeling but her feelings are usually right.

Joey is standing next to the fort in the darkness, just outside of the glow of the neighbor's yellow hue porch light, his Walkman clipped to his belt and the headphones around his neck. Joey won't go into the cabana alone; he's still convinced people were murdered there.

"Wuz up, little douche?" Joey asks with a cigarette dangling out of his mouth.

"Fuck you, Jo-Jo. Did you see Bear?" Lance asks as he reaches for Joey's cigarette. Joey tilts his head just out of reach and Lance whiffs the steal.

"No, why? Are you bringing the little monster?" Joey asks.

Joey and Bear don't get along. Joey is pretty rough with Bear when he tries to play with him, and Lance thinks Bear doesn't realize it's play. It usually ends with Bear growling or biting Joey.

"Yes…" Before he can finish, a dark figure emerges behind Joey from behind the cabana, and for a split-second Lance's heart skips a beat and fear engulfs him. His wide eyes must have startled Joey. Joey spins around with his hand already in his front pocket digging his knife out.

"You fucking dick!" Joey yells louder than he wanted. It's Jeremy holding Bear.

Lance is confused and happy that Jeremy is here, but still a little angry.

"What are you doing here? I thought you didn't have the stomach for it," Lance chides.

"After you and Joey both called, I knew I had to come. We have to save Ryan," he says as he sets Bear on the ground.

"I'm not going to lie. I was pretty pissed at you. In fact, I wasn't going to ever call you again. Well, if I survived that is. But, let bygones be bygones, I'm happy you're here, we need you," Lance says.

"Fucking kiss and get on with it already, fags. We got to go, yo," Leave it to Joey to break up an awkward moment with an awkward comment.

All three boys let out nervous laughs and start walking with Bear leading point. They walk shrouded by darkness toward the address Reno gave them, talking, and smoothing everything out between them. By the time they arrive, all three are back to normal, friends forever.

———

The house is pitch black. Reno's sister does not use nightlights. Even so, Reno can move freely about in the labyrinth. Her sister has more furniture and knick-knacks than anyone Reno knows. Reno has spent so much time here that she can navigate without sight.

A burglar would be tripping and falling as soon as he entered the house and the sound of dozens of porcelain and glass figurines smashing as they departed their dust-free shelves to the floor would surely wake everyone.

She's in the mint green guest bedroom and needs to make it to her sister's room down the hall to secure the car keys.

She silently slips down the hall, passing the all-pink bathroom.

Her sister loves pink and this bathroom is her shrine. The walls are pink, the bathtub, toilet, and sink are pink, the Formica countertop is pink with speckles, and even the carpet is pink. It's so pink that it almost glows.

She makes it to the bedroom and luck is on her side; the door is ajar. Reno drops onto all fours on the carpet and enters like a cat. Unfortunately, the keys are in a red carnival-glass bowl on the nightstand, right next to her sister's head. She takes a breath and holds it in as she reaches for the keys. The slight sound of metal against glass makes her cringe. Under normal circumstances, someone would really have to be focused to hear the *clink*, but tonight is not normal. Reno's sister doesn't stir, probably the Valium. With the keys secured tightly in her hand, she backtracks and goes to the kitchen.

Damn it, I forgot the note, she thinks.

She looks around the cluttered but clean kitchen for a notebook and pen. She has to leave a note, if not, her sister will think she was kidnapped and whoever abducted her also stole her car.

She finds a scrap piece of paper and a pen and scribbles a note that she is safe, but needs to borrow her car, and don't tell Mom or call the police.

She signs it with her signature autograph—a capital 'D' with a small 'r' nesting inside. Her signature reminds her of a cartoon ear, somehow, and she thinks it's cute.

The boys arrive just as Reno is attempting to slowly and quietly close the front door. She has not turned around so she doesn't see them and the porch light is off.

Her sister believes in conserving energy and water but is no longer an activist like she used to be. She attended a climate protest in San Francisco a few years ago and was almost arrested. She loves the Earth but not enough to go to jail.

Joey sees Reno's back is turned and can't help himself. He creeps up the driveway using the bushes as cover, ignoring Lance and Jeremy pulling on his arm. He grabs her around her waist and she lets out a blood-curdling scream as she simultaneously spins around and launches a fist full of keys into Joey's temple. All four of them instinctively crouch, wild-eyed, and spooked. Once Reno realizes it's Joey, she gestures a sigh of relief and then, "You're dead," she whispers as her hand rakes across her throat to give Joey a visual in case he didn't hear her.

They all regroup on the side of the house where it's dark and they can talk.

Over mild objections, Reno explains to the boys that she will be the only one driving. The car is her sister's baby and if it gets so much as a scratch, her sister will kill her. She also makes it clear that no eating or drinking will be allowed.

She picks up Bear and asks him, "Are you potty-trained, big guy?"

Bear licks her face in acknowledgment.

During all of this Lance is wondering, *What kind of car does her sister own? Must be a Lambo. It better be a Lambo the way she's acting and not some piece of crap.* Lance would not know a piece of crap from a muscle car.

They finalize their plan and set it in motion. Reno will get in the car and put it in neutral. The boys will push it out of the driveway and down the street far enough that her sister won't hear it start. Simple.

The night is warm and the air fresh. The mountains to the north are voluminous and dark. The stars in the sky shimmer dim and distant, clouds obstructing much of the view. The street has no street lights and only a couple of random houses have their porch lights on. It's a perfect night to steal a car and attempt to break into Sheol.

Lance looks skyward and can't believe they *are* actually stealing a car. He's torn. He knows that this is wrong, but he knows that they must do it if they are going to save Ryan. He wonders about his partners in crime and what they must be thinking. He knows Joey doesn't care; he's more of a daredevil and fly-by-the-seat-of-his-pants type of person. This whole situation has to be weighing heavily on Jeremy. Under no other circumstances would he attempt something like this, and he doesn't want to be here to begin with. Reno is hard to figure out and Lance is wondering why she is going along with any of it. She has no skin in the game. Maybe she's bored or going to her dad's house is so bad she would rather end up in juvenile detention or worse. Or, maybe Reno doesn't really understand what she's getting herself into. *That must be it*, Lance thinks.

Reno slides behind the steering wheel of her sister's car—a blue and white, 1976 Ford Mustang Cobra II—and puts the transmission in neutral. The boys creep to the front of the vehicle and begin pushing. All three of them are excited because the car looks cool and fast and their adrenaline is pumping. They push the car a full block before stopping, all of them now sweating from their pit crew work. Reno should have steered the car to the left, downhill, not right. The boys calmly climb into the two-door and sit quietly in suspense waiting for Reno to start the car.

"You know how to drive?" Jeremy asks, holding Bear in his lap.

"Of course, don't be stupid," Reno fires back. "I just have to remember which key is the car key. There're so damn many."

After fiddling with the keys, she finally hits the jackpot and the car roars to life. Now it's real. They are actually going to do this. All of them are in it together.

Lance says a little prayer in his head asking God to guide and protect them. He knows he has Emma on his side, and he really thinks that she is an angel of God, but speaking directly to the Big Man can't hurt and they will need all of the help they can get.

It takes Reno a couple of blocks to figure out how to turn the headlights on and Jeremy notices that she hasn't used her blinkers once. He hopes that she starts or they run the risk of getting pulled over. He was about to mention that to her, but Joey beat him to the punch.

"Yo, Reno, you might want to try the little handle by the steering wheel, it turns on the blinkers. Down for left, and up for right. I thought you said you know how to drive."

"Joey, shut up, which way? You're supposed to be the navigator. You do your job and let me do mine," Reno says, obviously somewhat annoyed. She's the one risking everything—running away, stealing her sister's car, and driving without a license. When she told the boys that she knows how to drive she failed to mention that all of her driving time was out in the country with her mom in the passenger seat. At this point she doesn't care. There's no way she is going to risk damage to her sister's car by letting one of these buffoons behind the wheel. Her sister loves *Charlie's Angels* and bought the car because of the show. The car is her pride and joy and Reno feels bad about "borrowing" it without her consent.

"Damn, I don't know. It's too dark and I can't see the map." In truth, even if Joey could see the map he wouldn't know. He's never read a map. Plus, he never volunteered to be the navigator so in his mind, they shouldn't expect much. He's already irritated that Reno won't let him drive and now she expects him to be Johnny-on-the-spot.

"Take a right and follow Eagle road up to I-84. We need to be going west on the freeway to get to Oregon," Jeremy explains to Reno. He's been to Ontario, Oregon quite a few times. His brother, Brian, had a girlfriend in Ontario and Jeremy would go with him until they broke up. He misses his brother already and hopes that he survives and gets to see him.

Twenty minutes later, they are on I-84 heading westbound. Spirits in the car are high and they all believe it should be easy sailing from here. They did not realize that a quarter of a tank of gas does not get you very far.

CHAPTER 4

ASS. GAS. OR GRASS.
NOBODY RIDES FOR FREE

lack, clack, clack. The dreaded sound of running out of gas. It rings from the engine bay into the cabin. At first, all four of the occupants freeze in place and then start looking at each other as if one of them will know what the sound means, which of course, none of them do. Then the car starts stuttering and jerking.

"What's happening?" Reno asks no one in particular, just hoping for an answer. She gets no help from the boys, not because they don't want to help, but because they don't know what's happening.

Reno glides the car to the skinny shoulder of the freeway and they come to a complete stop. As soon as she puts the car in park, Joey jumps out and heads to the front moving with confidence. Sometimes Joey's ego gets the better of him.

"Pop the top," he says as he gives the hood two firm smacks.

"How? Is there a button or something?" Reno yells out the window expecting Joey to know.

He doesn't, so he can't answer. He pretends that he didn't hear her.

Luck is on their side because the freeway is deserted. If someone sees them parked on the shoulder, they may stop to offer help and once they realize it's a bunch of kids, they could call the police.

"Reno, look down by your left leg. There should be something to pull to pop the hood," Jeremy offers.

"Maybe it's just out of gas," Lance says. He has no basis for his explanation but for some reason it just sounded right in his head. "Where's the needle on the gas gauge?"

Reno looks around the cluster of gauges just above the steering wheel and finally figures out which one is the gas. "The needle is on 'E.' What does that mean?"

"It means we're screwed, that's what that means," Jeremy says in a deflated tone.

Every minute they sit on the side of the road they risk getting caught.

"What do we do? Joey, get back in here we're out of gas!" Reno yells out the window again.

It's well past 1:00 a.m.; it's dark, and they are basically out in the middle of nowhere. They need to decide what to do and they need to do it fast. They all start to throw out ideas, but every time there's an idea, someone in the group shoots it down. They are getting nowhere in their circular conversation and tempers are starting to rise. All of them feel helpless and agitated.

Lance knows that if they don't figure something out soon, Jeremy and Reno will probably vote to go back home and forget the mission. He needs to take charge and steer the conversation to a suitable resolution and he knows he's running out of time. *Operation Rescue Ry-Ry* might be over before it really starts. He runs a couple of different scenarios through his head before settling on one he rejected earlier. He doesn't see any other option.

"Let's hitchhike to Baker," he blurts out, not really expecting any of them to agree but knowing that he has to come up with anything other than going back home.

"I'm down," Joey says as he fishes out a cigarette from the crumpled pack in the zippered pocket of his black parachute pants.

Lance knew Joey would agree. It sounds dangerous and exciting. Heck, they might get picked up by a van full of hippies with weed, or on the flip side, a serial killer. Lance wasn't worried about Joey; it's the other two he knows he has to convince.

"Think about it. We can lock the car so no one breaks into it. It'll be safe right here until we get back."

Lance didn't know that the car would get marked with a big orange checkmark and twenty-four hours later it would be towed. Reno's sister will have to pay for the tow and storage once notified.

"And, we will only get into a car that feels safe. Maybe a family on vacation will come by and pick us up." He's looking around at them in the dark. "Come on guys. We need to make a decision. I think we're close to Baker City. I know we're too close to turn back."

He is pleading because he knows that Jeremy wants nothing more than to turn around and go back to his boring life fighting with his brother.

None of this feels *right* or *good* to Jeremy and he is again second guessing his decision to let his emotions and loyalty to his friends override his common sense. Jeremy also knows that being so close to Lance is dangerous. Charlie needs both of their blood to merge Adamah and Sheol. Charlie can't do it with just one, it won't work. If he stays in Adamah and Lance goes to Sheol they will be separated and that makes Charlie's job much harder. But Jeremy reluctantly agrees instead of breaking Lance's heart.

Reno is the last one and Lance knows she's still not sold. "Reno, I promise your sister's car will be fine right here. I see cars on the side of the freeway all the time."

Lance is lying. The few times he's been on the freeway he has yet to see an abandoned car. He tries his best to flash Reno a confident, and maybe even a sexy, grin.

Reno doesn't believe Lance, and she's not sure what he's trying to do with that awkward smile, but she knows how much finding Ryan means. She knows Lance doesn't know it, but she really likes him. He's cute, quirky, honest, and genuinely a good person.

"Okay, but only if you're sure it will be safe. You know that this car is my sister's everything. It will kill her if anything happens to it. You promise?"

Lance knows that if he says 'yes' he will be lying to her, and he likes her too much to lie, so he reluctantly says, "I can't promise, but I think it will be okay and what other option do we have? Please Reno."

She agrees and they immediately start preparing.

As Lance grabs his backpack, he can't ignore the nagging feeling in his head that this really isn't a good idea.

Emma, you here? Are we doing the right thing?

Radio silence. Lance is confused. He thought she was always with him especially now when he really needs her. Did something happen that he doesn't know? Is there some reason why she's not with him right now?

Emma *is* still with Lance, but Lance needs to be able to make decisions on his own and not always rely on her. When he really needs her, when the time comes, she will be there.

They've been walking in the dark for about thirty minutes and all of them are starting to get tired. It didn't dawn on any of them to take a nap before their big night. No one is talking, not even Joey. They just keep walking and walking. Not one car has gone by.

Lance wonders if he made the right decision for his group and the whole situation is beginning to feel dismal. He scoops Bear up into his arms to give the little guy a break. He knows if he is tired then Bear has to be tired especially because it takes Bear a lot more effort with his short legs to keep up. Bear locks eyes with Lance and Lance wishes he could communicate so they could understand each other like how he communicates with Emma. He looks at Jeremy and notices Jeremy's posture is the same as it was before he left the cabana: shoulders slumped and head down. He hopes Jeremy will be able to make this journey. He needs him. If for nothing else, he needs him for support.

Amy is slowly walking down a dark street about five blocks from their hunting ground—the overpass. She's already been there and had to leave. She's tired of the homeless. They stink and repulse her. She wants someone higher on the societal ladder tonight, maybe a person that showered in the last twenty-four hours and whose breath doesn't smell like booze or rot. She left Ryan and didn't bother telling him, not like he cares either way. The further she gets from the overpass, the better her mood. The evening is early so she has all night to hunt and seduce her prey. She's going to take her time and pick a good one.

Two teenage Latino boys are sitting on the steps of a Catholic church when she walks by them. They've been there for about an hour drinking Mad Dog 20/20 and at this point are pretty wasted. The older boy is tall and chunky and his younger counterpart is short and stout. Everyone calls them Foghorn Leghorn and Chicken Hawk. The young one sees Amy first.

"Yo, mama you lookin good," he cat-calls to her as he grinds his elbow into the older boy's ribs who looks up from picking his big toenail. The bigger one smiles at her and rubs his fingers under the younger boy's nose and laughs.

"Jorge, what the fuck is wrong with you, nasty puta," Chicken Hawk yells as he jumps up from the step and blocks Amy's path. "Damn chica you arrre fine." He whistles.

Jorge stands and slides his foot into his cheap flip-flops and jumps down next to his partner so he can get a better look.

"Yeah, mama, you are fine. You want to party?" he says, shaking the half bottle of 20/20.

On a normal night Amy would shred these two punks and stuff their balls into their mouths. But tonight is not a normal night. She's in a good mood so she decides to give them a chance to save themselves. She can smell the boys and knows that hygiene is not a priority and their booze breath is angering her.

"Boys, you really don't want to do this. Your odor is putting me in a bad mood," she says as she pinches her perfect cosmetically altered nose.

"Bitch, you sayin' we stink? You're going to smell real bad when we skull fuck you to death," little Chicken Hawk says as he moves to her side like he's going to try and grab her from behind.

At that moment a brown Toyota Corolla turns the corner and the driver, Dave, sees the three on the sidewalk and realizes what is about to happen. He slams on the brakes and comes to a screeching halt. He is a big man, about six-foot, and he's wearing a black Oakland Raiders baseball cap turned backward. His long brown hair nearly reaches his shoulders. He jumps out of the car and before he can even say a word, Foghorn and Chicken Hawk take off running down the sidewalk and turn into an alley.

"You okay, miss?" Dave asks, staring down the sidewalk in the direction of the vanished boys.

"I am now," Amy says as she sizes up Dave as her new victim. He's tall, handsome, and smells good. Just what she wanted.

Too bad for him, he's in the wrong place at the wrong time. He was trying to do what he thought was a good deed and it might unknowingly cost him his life.

"It looked like those kids were up to no good. A girl as pretty as you should not be walking around this neighborhood alone. I'm Dave by the way."

"I'm Amy," she says. She has made up her mind that this is the one. She noticed that Dave is not wearing a wedding ring. "You married or have a girlfriend?"

"I have a girlfriend, but she's in California visiting her family. I know this is kind of forward, but would you want to go have a drink or come over to my place?"

"I would love to but I'm working right now."

"Working? Where do you work?"

"Right here. Well, actually about two blocks over. Men pay me to go out with them." She winks at him and flips her hair over her shoulder.

Normally, Amy wouldn't pretend to be a prostitute. The degenerates under the overpass wouldn't have a nickel to their name. But tonight she's feeling frisky and this guy looks like he can afford it and she feels like playing.

Dave breaks out with a big grin. "I get it. How much do you charge? It has to be a lot as pretty as you are."

"Since you saved my life, I'll give you a discount. How about a Benji for a full ride?"

"So, what does that mean?"

"Let me be blunt. For a hundred bucks, I'll fuck you."

"Let's go. Do you have a place or do you want to go to my apartment?"

"My place, it's about a quarter mile down the road," she says as she slides into the passenger seat of the Toyota.

As soon as they pull out the flashing blue lights of a Ford LTD Crown Victoria bounce off the buildings on the narrow street. The police officer watched the altercation with the young boys and then the exchange of money between Amy and Dave. He thinks they made a drug deal and wants to search the car. Plus, Amy looks stunning and he really wants to pat her down. Maybe she will be willing to exchange a service for her freedom. It's not the first time the eight-year veteran has helped out his community this way.

Now Amy is pissed. This is not how tonight was supposed to play out. God help these two pitiful unknowing bastards.

The cop places Amy and Dave in handcuffs and sits them on the curb. He told them they are not under arrest, just detained for his safety until he can figure out what happened. He stands Dave up, who hovers above him by a good four inches and places him in the back of his cruiser. Then he turns his attention to Amy.

"Ma'am, I'm going to have to pat you down to make sure you don't have any illegal drugs or weapons hiding in that tight skirt." He smirks, visibly excited.

The cop stands her up and starts his search. First, her lady bumps. His hands linger on her firm breasts and he leans in closer to her. So close his crotch is rubbing against her butt.

He moves his hands down her sides and across her abdomen and notes how firm her stomach feels. The cop spins her around and starts over down her backside and his hands rest on her rock-hard buttocks. Amy's eyes are level with his badge so he does not see the hatred brewing inside her. Even if he did, he would not care. He's done this many times before and they all comply and no one has ever filed on him. One, because they are ashamed and embarrassed. Two, because he threatens them when he's done and had his way.

He lifts her short skirt and notices her underwear matches her bra and he likes that. He sees a bulge that should not be there and fishes it out. A little brown leather wrap.

"Hmm, what do we have here?" he says as he unrolls the package. It's a syringe with an orange cap and a little vial of heroin.

"Tell you what sweetie, if you do me a favor, I'll let you and your friend go tonight. No reason to go to jail and I don't feel like doing the paperwork. What do you think?"

He knows he has her now.

"What do you have in mind?" she asks.

"Give me a BJ and all of this never happened."

"You have to take my cuffs off of me so I can stroke it," she says, looking up at him and licking her glossy red lips.

"Good try, but no. The cuffs stay on until we're done. If your friend is into it, he can watch."

Ryan appears next to the cop seemingly out of thin air and Amy sees him first. She cracks a wicked smile. Ryan summons his new partner without speaking a word. A shadow specter appears behind the cop and wraps its long black fingers around his neck and places its knee on the small of his back and leans back. Way back. The cop's vertebrae snaps like a twig releasing a gruesomely loud *craack* and an equally morbid scream from his mouth. When his spine snapped, it instantly killed him. His lower body fell toward Amy while his upper torso fell back looking up toward the sky. The force was so violent the poor cops stomach split wide open.

"We have to go; Charlie wants us back. He said we need to be ready to go to another portal when he summons us." Ryan directs Amy.

As they leave the grisly scene Amy is disappointed she did not get to kill the cop, but she thinks she still has Dave. She walks to the cop car and her smile turns to a frown. The rear windows are pasted with flesh and blood. She doesn't need to see inside to know that Dave is already dead. The shadow specter made quick work of him, too. Ryan and Amy silently walk back to the drug den to await Charlie's order. Ryan is glad that he did not have to kill them with his own hands.

Another thirty minutes go by when Joey suddenly spins around on his heels and starts pointing. "Look, a car. A fucking car is finally coming. The son-of-a-bitch better stop for us."

Instantly, everyone gets a shot of adrenaline, even Jeremy, and they all perk up.

"Safe at last, safe at last, thank you baby Jesus, we are safe at last!" Joey is yelling at the car. "Shit, we need to signal or it's going to zip right past us. What do we do?"

He looks at Lance. Lance doesn't have a clue. He doesn't answer. Reno suddenly jumps into the car's lane and starts cycling her flashlight on-off-on-off. It's still coming in hot and all of them think the worst. It's going to drive right past them. It suddenly starts to slow down a couple of hundred feet behind them. As it creeps closer, they can make out that it's a van or pickup truck. When it finally stops about twenty feet from them, the headlights temporarily blind them but it's definitely a van.

Of course, Joey says out loud what all of them are thinking.

"Fuck, it's a chomo van. I hope there's not a child molester in there," he says as he fishes his pocket knife out and flicks the blade open twisting it up to hide it behind his hand and wrist.

In the back of Joey's mind, there's a little part of him that hopes the driver is a chomo so he can use his blade to teach him a lesson. The van creeps closer and comes to a rest next to the kids.

The driver leans over and rolls down the passenger window. "You need help?"

"Yeah, do you have any gas?" Lance asks, trying to get a better look inside the van. It's a brown 70s panel van so it does not have windows other than the driver and passenger doors, and its dark inside.

"No, little buddy, I don't have any gas. Is that what's wrong? You kids run out of gas?"

"Yes, do you have room in there to give us a ride to Baker City?" Lance asks as the other kids are looking over the exterior of the van trying to decide if it's safe. Both Lance and Joey think to themselves that if needed, all of them could take this one man. He doesn't look very big, but they haven't seen him standing.

"Yeah, of course, jump in. My name's Carter," the man says. He smiles.

All of the kids go through their own quick mental assessment and decide that he's safe and Joey opens the side door. The inside of the van looks normal. A few buckets, some tools scattered on the floor, and a big roll of plastic, the kind you use to put down on the floor when painting walls. Joey crawls to the passenger seat while the rest settle in the back.

"Bear come on, boy. Jump in," Reno calls.

Bear looks at her and whimpers but does not move to get in the van.

"Whoa, you kids got a dog? I don't usually allow animals in the Love Machine. Can you leave it with the car?"

"No, Bear comes with us. He's potty trained and won't bother you. How far is Baker from here anyways?" Lance asks as he gets out to pick up Bear.

"About fifty or sixty miles is my guess," Carter replies.

Bear is backing up as Lance advances and Lance thinks, *What is wrong with Bear? He never acts like this.* "Come on boy, we have to go."

He finally corrals him and scoops him up in his arms and crawls back into the van. As soon as he loosens his grip, Bear makes a break for the door. Reno swings it closed just in time. Trapped, Bear begins running around the back of the van sniffing, and Carter pulls out onto the freeway.

"So, why are you kids going to Baker? Seems kind of odd this late at night and all," Carter asks, hoping they make up some bullshit story.

He knows that kids driving in the middle of the night without an adult are up to something. Hell, they didn't even make sure they had gas. Staring straight ahead, but glancing in the rearview mirror, Carter starts to get excited but he doesn't show it, and he hopes the kid in the passenger seat can't see his little chub growing between his legs.

What the kids don't know *will* kill them. They got into a van in the middle of the night with what Joey was hoping for: a chomo.

"To meet Diana's dad, he's a cop over there and he was expecting us about an hour ago so he'll be worried," Joey explains, looking back at Lance and giving him a secret wink that Carter sees. "Lance and Diana are boyfriend/girlfriend and her dad wants to meet his future son-in-law," Joey finishes satisfied with himself that if this guy is a murderer he'll think twice.

"Wow, okay then, I need to get you kids there as quick as I can, safe and sound," Carter says, smiling. *Fucking ridiculous, this little snot nosed kid is going first.*

They drive for about twenty-five minutes when Carter decides that it's time. He's concocted a plan in his head to get all of the kids and that damn dog out of the van and he's going take the snot-nosed kid and have his way with him.

Carter starts kneading the gas pedal making the van lurch.

"Damn, I think somethings wrong with Gee-Gee," he says, still kneading the pedal.

"What's wrong? You run out of gas too?" Joey asks.

"No, kid. I think I'm running out of blinker fluid," he says, trying not to laugh out loud, looking around expecting one of them to call him out on his bullshit. But, when they don't, he keeps going. "Fuck, I have to pull over and check it. Oh well, it will give us all a chance to stretch and go to the bathroom. Make sure that dog gets out too. I don't want it pissing in my van," he says, pulling off the road and parking, leaving the van running. *Good none of them asked why I left it on.* "Alright kids, get out and stretch."

They all get out and look around. It's pitch black and barren desert. They stretch and the three boys walk to the back of the van to piss while Reno takes Bear further off the road into a little gully for some privacy.

"He's not bad. That's a good thing," Joey says to Jeremy and Lance.

"Yeah, I guess, but I have a weird feeling about him. If he offers us alcohol or drugs turn it down," Jeremy answers back.

When they get done, they all start walking in the direction Reno went to make sure she's alright.

"Kid, can you come over here and help?" Carter calls out to Joey. All three boys turn around and he points at Joey.

They figure it's safe. Joey is a guy and if he does need help, they can be over there in a matter of seconds. Joey spins on his heels and starts walking back toward the van.

"Yep, it's the blinker fluid, just as I thought," Carter says not hiding his shit-eating grin in the dark. "Can you grab me a can? It's in the back of the van. Should be around the big tool box."

"Sure, what color is it?" Joey is already in the van on his knees when Carter jumps in and slams the door shut. He begins punching Joey in the back of the head as hard as he can trying to knock him out long enough to get his handcuffs on him.

Bear hears Joey's scream and is growling and running toward the van. When he gets there, he helplessly claws at the door, barking and crying. The other kids run toward the van, yelling for Joey as the vehicle peels out and disappears into the darkness.

Carter knows that the kid will come-to fairly quick if he didn't accidentally kill him. He hopes not; that would be such a waste.

Joey regains consciousness almost immediately after being hit, but it takes him a few seconds to get his bearings.

Fuck, I'm going to die, he thinks as he fishes his knife out of his pocket and opens the blade, the only problem is his hands are cuffed.

Charlie and Joey share a special connection. They have ever since their first meeting at the Thriftway building and Charlie needs him to trap the other boys.. Lance has Emma and now Joey has…It's not Charlie, or a groupling. It's a specter that Charlie has charged with leading the boys back to him. Like Emma, it can communicate with Joey in his head and take on a physical form but only for a short time. It's too taxing if its more than a few seconds.

Carter can hear Joey talking out loud to someone and the first thing that flashes in his head is one of the other kids snuck into the van, but the voice isn't right. It belongs to a man. He turns and looks into the back of the van and it's black. There's nothing. He focuses back on the road ahead and wonders if he imagined it, but the voice felt so real. He glances in the rearview mirror and sees

Joey and something or someone staring back at him. He knows someone else is there with Joey and he gets chills down his arms and an acute flash of red as the blood rushes his brain preparing to go into flight or fight mode. It scares him so bad that he slams on the brakes and the force drives the steering wheel into his chest, knocking the wind out of him and that's Joey's chance.

I'm going to teach this motherfucker a lesson. You don't ever, ever, mess with Jo-Jo, especially if you're a fucking chomo. Joey lunges to the front seat and jams the same blade that killed Ryan into Carter's neck and twists.

Carter clutches his neck. His life is cycling in fast-motion before his eyes, his life and that horrific image in the rearview mirror will be the last thing he sees. Carter is in no condition to fight back and Joey's adrenaline soars as he cusses at Carter and opens the driver's side door. He punches him a couple of times in the face before pushing him out onto the ground.

The voice calmly asks him if that's all he wants to do to this chomo.

"No, no it's not," he says and leaps out and begins violently kicking him.

The voice is not satisfied, it knows it has to push Joey if it wants to take hold of him. It barks orders, morbid orders, that Joey follows. Carter will die in the dirt. His eyes will be ripped out of their sockets and stuffed down his throat. But Joey and his new friend are not done. Joey listens to the voice and pulls Carter's 501's down around his ankles and deflowers the mortally wounded man. He cuts his balls out of his ball sack and stuffs one in each gaping eye crevice. He stands to admire his gruesome handiwork. This chomo breathed his last useless breath and Joey is glad he is the one that took it. Joey jumps into the driver's seat and heads back toward the other kids, his parachute pants and black muscle shirt soaking up Carter's blood. He doesn't even notice that his handcuffs are off.

Joey returns to where the other kids are waiting. Other than a headache, he's fine and assures all of them that he can drive. He leaves out the part about the voice ordering him to mutilate Carter's body.

Lance is the only one that notices a difference in him. It's the same feeling he had following Joey up the stairs in the Thriftway Building Center the night they met Charlie. He doesn't say anything, but he knows Charlie is back.

All the kids and Bear pile into the van and continue west toward Baker City.

The police won't find Carter's body for another three days and they will never find his killer. Four years later, in 1988, they will match his DNA to two murder–rapes of adolescent boys that disappeared in Oregon.

As soon as the kids turn down a dirt road with tall dead trees flanking both sides and a decrepit barbwire fence, Joey can see the huge fading ranch style sign high above the road that reads, PINK HOUSE SWINE PROCESSING FARM, in pink letters, he starts in.

CHAPTER 5

SLAUGHTERHOUSE BLUES OR SIN CITY

"Hell no, Lance!" Joey blurts out, "don't tell me we're going into that creepy fucking place." Pointing, dry blood still spattered on his arms.

"This place is abandoned," Joey says, as he surveys the slight rolling hills peppered with small, neglected wood buildings that are capped with rusted tin roofs. All of them brandish barely visible building numbers, painted long ago in white. The road leads to the main slaughterhouse that sits atop the hill. It was once the pride and joy of the large operation, now it's relinquished to mother nature's brutal mood swings. Its shell is a mix of aged wood and tin sheets used as patches through the years, all of it held together by rusty nails. On the side of the building is a ginormous playful pink pig winking at all who enter. The roof is the same as the smaller buildings, and it has four cement loading docks and several chutes to herd the little piglets inside. If all of that isn't enough to convince Joey not to keep going, the black clouds and crack of thunder in the east do the trick.

Visibly sweating and agitated, Joey is trying to rub the itchy, dried blood off his arms as he continues his contentious argument that Lance has yet to join.

"It's going to be morning soon and I don't think any of us want to be here at night. Plus, it's going to rain. Why don't we wait for light?" Joey asks looking around, pleading with anyone who will agree.

Bear is the only one that seems the slightest bit interested and walks over to Joey and lies between his legs to try and calm him. Reno and Jeremy don't speak but they also agree with Joey; this place is creepy and will only get creepier when the storm hits.

Lance wants to agree with Joey and leave this place until morning now that they know where it is, but where will they go? Plus, he knows that the portal Emma told him about might not be here in the morning.

It's not like they can get into their comfy beds at home and start again tomorrow. No, they are already here and the quicker they can find the portal, the better.

"What do you guys think? Should we go in tonight or find a place to park and sleep until light?" Lance queries the group. "Remember, we're runaways in a stolen van and the owner is back there somewhere hurt."

He doesn't know Joey murdered Carter, none of them do.

Joey has an epiphany and changes direction mid-stream, guiding his canoe in the same direction as Lance.

Damn, he's right, what if they find the chomo? The gory image of Carter's bloody body with his balls crammed into his eye sockets is branded into his mind.

"We can't chance it. As much as I want to wait, we can't chance it. If Carter finds help and turns us in the police will know we were heading to Baker in his van. Let's go in," Joey says as he cringes inside, his stomach revolting the way it did last summer when a double-dog dare was laid at his feet to jump his Diamondback bike off the steep cliff by the ponds.

"It's settled then. We keep going." His spidey senses are tingling. Joey murdered Carter and is lying to them. There's more, Lance just hasn't figured it out yet.

They slowly creep up to the main building, the van's headlights shine a dreary yellow to match the mood of the occupants inside it.

Below the kid's feet, the rough, cracked concrete floor meant to keep the pigs' blood from soaking into the environment is stained with the tens of thousands of swine that met their final, inconsequential fate in this very spot.

Lance and Reno's flashlights are the only source of limited light dancing in front of them as they sweep the haunting room and the light brings none of them any comfort as the imaginary killer clown in their heads is handing out free passes to this nightmare. As if on cue, Thor crashes his hammer down on the rusty tin roof producing a thunderous clap followed by a torrential downpour. All of the kids jump out of their skin and Lance drops his flashlight. The rain flowing through the countless rusted holes in the roof forming small puddles inside the building. Bear is barking and whimpering, frightened by the deafening noise.

A sweeping chill fills the room and engulfs the kids as Joey's specter leads them to the portal. The same apparition that Carter saw in the rearview mirror. Joey is the only one that knows they have company.

"Come on, follow me," Joey yells in his best big boy voice. He is following his new friend as it calmly directs them past the scald tanks and scraping tables toward the back of the room. The others are oblivious to the fact that there is something else in the room, well almost everyone.

Lance is trailing behind the group. He took a few extra seconds to try and find his flashlight, no luck. When Reno's light passes over Joey, Lance can sense something is leading him. He is almost sure he sees a figure, but isn't certain. The room is too dark and the angles from the rain reflecting off the light beam distorts his view.

They follow Joey up a small flight of metal grate stairs into an office overlooking the kill floor. The windows are long gone but at least there is no rain in here. They have to speak loudly; the rain has not let up its battering crusade to finally break the roof's spirit.

"Holy shit, good God, it's got to be a sign. He doesn't want us here," Jeremy says as he tries to shake the water from his body imitating Bear.

Still upset that he lost his flashlight Lance fires back, "It's not a sign. Don't be ridiculous." He turns his attention to poor Bear. His dog is cold and has to be hungry, but he's a trooper and will follow Lance until he can no longer stand or simply falls over dead.

"Does anyone know where the portal is in here?" Jeremy surveys the group. "Why couldn't we just use the same one Charlie took us through at the Thriftway Building Center?"

This time he's specifically speaking to Lance and Jeremy.

"Emma told me the Thriftway portal moved. She said the portals are not permanent and that's why we had to hurry here to this one. But I don't know exactly where it's at," Lance answers.

"How will we know when we find it?" Reno wipes the cold rainwater off her forehead.

Lance looks out the glassless window down onto the kill floor and hopes that the animals that died, died without pain. It makes him contemplate never eating meat again.

"It has to be a door or entry, or something. We have to stick together. If we split up and randomly start opening doors one of us might cross over and the rest of us will never find them," he finally says.

"Sounds like a plan," Reno answers. "Should we wait for the rain to stop before we go traipsing around a slaughterhouse?"

"I vote yes," Joey says with his hand raised like he's in Mr. Tolsen's math class, in no hurry to leave the relative safety of the office. The others all nod their head in agreement.

While waiting, they all take time to reflect on what they've done so far and what might be before them in Sheol.

"Explain to me again about Charlie and this other world we're supposedly crossing into—Sheol?" Reno asks no one in particular.

Jeremy and Joey automatically look at Lance.

"Shit, what do you want to know?" Lance asks.

"Everything."

Lance details how Sheol is somehow a parallel world to theirs and that *something evil* (Erebus) wants to control both worlds and they are using Charlie to do it. He explains that Charlie was a murderer when alive and was handpicked by Erebus to converge the worlds.

"Charlie is a strange fellow, strange looking *and* acting, but don't let him fool you. He gets in your head and has some kind of charm that makes you want him to like you. He doesn't care about anyone or anything except himself." He looks at Joey with sorry eyes. "He made Joey kill Ryan right in front of us and laughed. He has powers, powers to make people do things they don't want to do and power to change things in Sheol."

Both Joey and Jeremy remember the horror Charlie put them through the last time they were in Sheol. If Joey was not so good at compartmentalizing his emotions, he would be in a nuthouse.

For Jeremy, it's even worse; he killed himself in Sheol and his once confident, strong, self is now as fragile as an eggshell. Internally, he's been trying to pull his former self out of a dark, locked closet in his mind. He can hear himself pounding on the door from the other side, but each time he tries to open it, it's deadbolted shut and his current self doesn't have the strength to free the real Jeremy. But Jeremy is a warrior and sooner or later he will break that damn door down.

Reno is hanging onto Lance's every word, and stealing glimpses at Jeremy and Joey who both look solemn and small. She notices that they both subconsciously worked their way to the far corner of the room up against the wall as if they are expecting Lance to yell *BOO* and scare them. Reno backs up and sits on the edge of the only desk in the room and crosses her legs, still listening intently.

"Sheol is another story. It's really weird. It looks like our world except everything has an orange tint. Charlie took us through an endless red desert and he could make a building appear out of nowhere. He has an army he calls grouplings. They aren't alive, but he can make them look and act normal. We watched them spoil and rot right before our eyes. Oh, and he can read your thoughts so he knows what you're thinking or about to do. The last time we were in Sheol, the ground started caving in all around us and his grouplings were everywhere... I forgot to mention the vultures," he says with a slight tinge of fear that was more noticeable than he wanted. "He has huge black vultures, the size of a short bus, but they don't have any feathers. Their bodies are black, cracking, and bald. Their heads, oh, their heads! No eyes. Only black sockets where their eyes should be, and they have row after row of sharp, long teeth. They remind me of shark teeth. He calls them whenever he wants and they come out of nowhere and swoop down to take people away somewhere, but we don't know where. I heard him call them highwaymen, but they're not human at all." One thing Lance has not been able to figure out is how Jeremy committed suicide in Sheol and returned to their world, Adamah, normal (sort of). If Ryan was murdered in Sheol how come he doesn't return to "normal" when he crosses back over? The only thing he can figure is Jeremy killed himself and Ryan was killed by someone else.

After Lance finishes talking and the room is silent except the rain striking the roof, Reno reflects on all that she has learned, the story in the cabana and just now.

It can't be real, she thinks.

She half expects them to run around this slaughterhouse for a few hours and then go home. Up to this point, she has not seen any grouplings or highwaymen, so she has no reason to believe any of it. But she did steal her sister's car, and drove all night to get here… So…maybe?

The rain suddenly stops as if Thor turned the handle to the faucet off. It was instantaneous and catches all of them by surprise. At first none of them say anything or move from their spots. Lance knows they have to hurry and find the portal, but does not want to move.

Reno says what the boys fear, "Sounds like the rain stopped. Should we get going? Who's in the lead?"

"I'll lead," Lance says as he moves toward the door of the office, flinging his backpack over his shoulders. Since they had time to think, Lance has been trying to figure out where the portal could be in this place. He knows it's here. Emma would not lie to him.

They all follow him out, Bear in the lead, and Jeremy in the back. There's a promising looking door on the other end of the kill floor, which is unlike any of the other doors. This one is painted red and from a distance it looks like someone threw a bucket of blood on it. The path to the door is not a straight shot; they have to bob-and-weave around upturned stainless-steel tables, saws, puddles, and broken boards littering the floor. Once in front of the door, Lance stops and turns around even before trying the handle to see if it's locked.

"If this is the portal, prepare yourself," he says to all of them. He scoops Bear into his arms and turns back around and turns the handle. "Damn it, it's locked." He hands Bear to Reno so he can use both hands and wrestles with the door for a couple of minutes. Joey is standing beside him with a large rusty iron pipe.

"Let a real man give it a shot, sonny," he says as he slams the pipe down onto the handle. The handle gives with ease and Joey gets a shit-eating grin on his face as he turns around waiting for the commoners to applaud his heroism. He gets none.

Lance pushes past him and rushes into the room. The others follow. They all stand in the center of what looks like a supply cage, bewildered.

"I thought for sure this was it," Lance says with a baffled look on his face. The room is barely big enough for all four of them to stand and all four walls have chain link fence around them. An old three-shelf storage rack runs the length of the back wall, leaning, ready to fall over. This is definitely not the portal.

They all back out of the room and as soon as Joey clears the door, he's jogging up the metal steps to another door that appears to lead to the outside. It's a metal double door.

"Let's try this one guys," he says once he reaches the top of the steps and looks back.

They all follow him and once everyone is in place, he turns the handle and kicks the door open. Nothing, but it does lead to the outside.

They try two more doors before Reno says, "I don't think it's here. At least not in this building. Maybe, we should try some of the smaller buildings we passed on the way up here. What do you guys think?"

"It's here, I know it is. Emma wouldn't tell me it's here if it wasn't," Lance replies, understanding the urgency. If they give up and leave, all of them will want to go home, so to placate Reno he says, "Okay, let's go check some of the other buildings, but if it's not there can we come back and make sure we didn't miss anything?"

They all nod in agreement and start walking toward the same door they entered during the storm. When they're about ten feet from the entrance, they hear a howl from outside; it sounds like a coyote or a wolf. All of them jump and then freeze, frightened by the sound. Bear leaps from Reno's arms, barking as he runs toward the swinging door, the handle long ago rusted and broken, ignoring Lance's commands to stop, to come back. They chase after him and plow through the door.

It's the portal and they all just crossed the threshold. Before anyone has a chance to say or do anything, Lance remembers how it happened with Charlie. The portal was the same door they opened to get to the roof of the Thriftway and when they came back through to escape the cowboy, they were in Sheol. It's not the door per se. It's being in the right place at the right time and crossing back the same way you enter.

At first, Reno thinks she's walked into a fire. The sky is orange and there is a sweltering dry heat prickling her skin and smacking her in the face. The sky is so bright that she shields her eyes as she shakes her head trying to clear it, dazed and confused.

What the hell just happened? she thinks as the terrifying realization overcomes her that *it happened.* She's in Sheol. *Please let this be a dream, please let this be a dream*, she says to herself or maybe to God.

When the boys cross over, they are overcome with mind-bending flashbacks of their last visit; the part of their brain associated with fear memories, the amygdala, is on fire. It is so emotionally overwhelming that they are physically drained of energy. All of them can feel the evil surrounding them. It feels like walking too close to a powerline and hearing the hum from above and electricity in the ground.

Lance is impacted the most. When he crossed over, he also had his first real vision of Ryan even if only for a second. It was like watching from a hidden camera in a ceiling.

Ryan was sitting on a dirty mattress next to a girl with his arm around her like he's consoling her. He leaned into her almost touching her head with his, her right hand on his thigh. What Lance did not know is Ryan just gave the girl a lethal dose of heroin and is waiting for her to expire; she will be a groupling.

Ryan looks up and for a brief nanosecond, Lance and Ryan lock eyes. Ryan is seeing his friend for the first time since his turning and it shocks Lance out of his vision. Ryan doesn't know what it means. He didn't even recognize Lance; his state as a groupling does not afford such luxuries.

"He's alive. Ryan is alive. When I went through the portal, I had a vision. He's sitting in a room with a girl, but I don't know where."

The other kids, either too tired or too scared, barely acknowledge him.

Joey had his own vision when he passed through the portal, but his was much darker. It was Charlie, and Charlie only said, *Bring them to me.*

Through all of the confusion and excitement, the kids did not even have a chance to look around at their surroundings. Jeremy is the first to notice that they are not at the slaughterhouse in Baker City, Oregon. In fact, they don't know where they are. They can see buildings off to the south surrounded by desert, but the kids are on a hill in the middle of nowhere. It reminds the boys of the red desert they traveled through for days the last time. The city below them is a couple of miles away and in this heat, walking will be slow going.

Lance pulls a blue Boy Scouts canteen out of his backpack and takes a swig and hands it to Jeremy. They pass the canteen around and when it gets back to Lance; he automatically kneels down to give Bear a drink, but Bear is nowhere in sight. Panic sets in and Lance is frantically calling his best friend and the other kids join in the search. After about five minutes they stop. They are out in the middle of nowhere so if Bear was near he would be easy to spot. Lance doesn't know what to do and is beside himself. He wants to cry, and he tries his best not to, but tears begin to bubble and it will only be a matter of seconds before they roll down his face.

During all of this, Reno has not stopped looking. She loves Bear as much as Lance, and she won't stop until they find him. She's about a hundred yards from the boys when they hear her yell for them. They all run toward her and she points to the ground. Lance fears she's pointing at his dog, dead lying in the dirt, but it's a hole, maybe from a badger or fox. It could even be a coyote den. And then they hear it: Bear barking.

How did he get down there? Lance wonders when he's close enough to see.

The entrance to the hole is caved in and Bear is stuck. Lance drops down to his knees and frantically begins shoveling dirt away. Bear's barking gets louder and louder. First, they see his snout, his wet nose covered in red dirt, and then he comes flying out the hole and into Lance's arms, safe. Lance scolds him in his baby voice and gives him a healthy drink from the canteen. The kids begin their long walk to the city below, hoping that is where Ryan will be found.

The sun's sweltering rays bounce off the hot asphalt and distort the city view. They're in Las Vegas, or Sheol's version of Las Vegas.

This is not a happy place, no bright lights, limousines, pretty women, or an abundance of money to be won or lost. Not here. Many of the buildings resemble the real Vegas, The Golden Nugget, The Dunes, Frontier, Stardust, and more, but these buildings are dilapidated. Many of the neon signs lay on the ground or are haphazardly secured to the facade, the bulbs long ago broken and never replaced. A few of the signs blink erratically, keeping tune to a psychotic rhythm nobody can hear. There is one building that stands out, Circus Circus. It looks as fresh as the day it was built. The neon winking in chorus invites all to come and enjoy what's inside; it's sure to be a fun time.

As the kids make their way through the streets, they observe something else that's strange: no cars are driving on the streets. There are plenty of cars parked alongside them and in the massive parking lots, but none are moving. They do see people coming in and out of the buildings and walking down the sidewalks, but they're odd. They are not talking or laughing, and they appear to walk without a purpose like they have nowhere to go, to be. The whole town has an eerie feeling like it's been overrun by zombies. As the kids get closer to a man walking by himself, he does not look up or acknowledge them in any way, simply passes by them. Bear's nose is working overtime and lets out a slight whimper as he dashes around to the other side of Lance, far from the passing man.

Reno is the first to notice it and says, "I don't want to be rude but that dude needs a shower. He stinks really bad. And is he missing his nose? And I did see green slime on his face like he's rotting, right?"

No answer from the boys.

She continues. "Is he part of a show or act in one of the casinos? My mom told me about the great shows here."

Jeremy, looking visibly shaken, finally answers her. "He's dead, real dead, not fake. He's a groupling, all of these people must be grouplings. We have to be careful. We should avoid them; they might be communicating with Charlie."

"Jeremy's right. We should get off the street and hide until we figure out where Ryan is. Circus Circus looks like the best place, let's go there," Lance says, still turned around, watching the groupling to make sure he doesn't double back.

Joey nods in agreement and already has his knife out, blade open. They take a side street where they feel there will be less activity and also gives them a better chance to run if needed. They arrive at Circus Circus and enter the building through the back. Lance notices that this place is the opposite of the gas station/diner they went to last time when Charlie had them. That place was rundown looking on the outside and brand-new inside. Circus Circus looks new outside and as he scans the inside, he can see it hasn't been operational in quite some time. All of the slot machines are off, some of them tipped over; the red felt on the card tables are ripped and stained, and the once bright carpet on the floor has met the same demise as the tables.

"Okay, now what?" Joey asks.

"I don't know. I just wanted us to get somewhere safe where we can think. We need to try and figure out where Charlie has Ryan," Lance answers, still looking around the vacant building. As he's scanning, he sees movement out of the corner of his eye and it startles him.

Lance didn't really see anybody. It was the specter showing himself to Joey, and Lance *felt* him.

The specter tells Joey that Ryan is not in this city. If they want to find him, they must go to the epicenter—the factory. Joey doesn't tell the others; he can't because he has to figure out a way to tell them without them figuring out he's being fed information from one of Charlie's underlings.

"I didn't see anything," he says, scanning the area that Lance is pointing, a corner of the slot machine area that's dark, darker than the rest of the building. All of the lights are out. Lance picks up a brass tube, a piece of railing that broke off long ago, and starts walking toward the corner where he thought he saw someone. Bear runs ahead sniffing and exploring everything in the room, doing what dogs do, which includes hiking his leg and peeing on a capsized Keno machine.

Nothing.

When they get to the corner, there is nowhere for someone to hide so Lance knows that he couldn't have seen anyone.

Bear starts growling and barking at a door about ten feet from where they are standing. Someone or something is in there. All of the kids immediately go on high alert and Jeremy produces a knife from his back pocket and flips the blade open. Reno pulls a six-inch fixed blade hunting knife from her purse.

Lance looks around at the three of them holding their knives and says, "Am I the only one that didn't bring a knife?"

He lets out a weak laugh as all of them stare back at him steely-eyed and serious. They begin moving toward the door, imagination running wild about what they will find on the other side.

Bear is still scratching and barking as Lance approaches. Reno hands him her knife and takes the brass tube.

Before he swings the door open, he thinks, *Can I really stab someone, kill someone?* But then he remembers he's in Sheol and grouplings are already dead, or undead… and can come back. He decides he can if it means saving himself and his friends.

"Reno, grab Bear. I don't want him to get hurt if there's something bad in here," he says as he simultaneously jerks the door open and closes his eyes for just a split second.

It's Joey's worst nightmare come true, a killer clown, or better put, a groupling dressed in a soiled and ripped Circus Circus clown costume standing in the middle of the hallway looking back at them. Joey is pretty sure the red around the clown's mouth is blood and not makeup.

He screams and retreats backward, tripping over one of the up-turned chairs and popping up with a frantic look on his face. Lance and Jeremy slam the door shut and start pushing a slot machine over to block it.

"We got to go, we got to go! Let's get the fuck out of here!" Joey yells, his voice cracking with fear. The others agree as they run toward the back of the casino, Joey leading the way. From the front there's a cacophony of broken glass and wood splintering as more grouplings flow into the casino. Once outside, the kids and Bear run across the parking lot. Grouplings seem to appear out of nowhere. It reminds the boys of their first journey when Charlie ordered his undead to converge on the factory.

Why aren't we taking one of these cars? Reno thinks, struggling to keep up, still holding Bear, abandoning the brass tube long ago.

She stops and tries the door handle of the next car she comes across. It just happens to be a black-on-black 1969 GTO Judge. Amazingly, the car starts and roars to life shooting black smoke out of its tailpipes, clearing its lungs, ready for the next road trip. She pulls up next to the boys who are still running and they give her a big smile and thumbs up as they all cram into the vehicle.

"Holy shit, this is cool. What is it?" Joey asks, squirming into the back seat behind her.

"I don't know, but it looks fast, and it's the first car I came to, so I tried it."

"Good job, Reno. It's a Pontiac GTO, the Judge. Brian has a poster on his wall of this same car, except it's orange," Jeremy says.

"Cool car, but now where are we going?" Lance asks, slightly deflating everyone's newfound enthusiasm.

Joey decides he has to tell the group what the specter told him in the casino. He just doesn't know how to do it without raising suspicion.

What Joey doesn't know is that it was the specter that summoned all of the grouplings that came crashing into the casino, hoping to capture the boys.

He decides to keep quiet and not say anything, at least for the time being.

They are outside the city limits now and entering the desert.

Reno, now keenly aware how important gas is to a running car, looks at the gas gauge. All of the gauges are pegged to the left, nothing registering. "Guys, I don't know how much gas this car has in it. None of the gauges are working."

"If it's anything like last time, we won't have to worry about it. For some reason, cars here don't need gas at least that we know," Lance says, glancing out the rearview mirror to see if they are being followed.

They are not; it's barren.

Why is it both times we are the only ones driving cars? he wonders.

The answer is simple. The grouplings don't have the mental capacity to drive. That's why all of the cars in Vegas sit vacant.

It's eating Joey up inside not being able to tell the others that Ryan is at the factory. He decides he just needs to come out with it. "I have a feeling that Ryan is at the factory, the one we escaped from the first time. Maybe, we should try there first."

"What makes you think that?" Reno asks.

"I don't know, it's just a feeling. It makes sense, sort of."

"Yeah, I guess it does make sense, but man, I don't want to go back to that place," Jeremy adds.

As the three of them discuss Joey's *feelings*, Lance is trying to have another conversation, but not with them, with Emma. He rubs the talisman hanging around his neck as he tries to shake the feeling of déjà vu, riding in the backseat of a car staring at a red desert heading toward some ungodly, evil place.

Emma, we really need your help right now. Where are you? Where is Ryan?

Nothing.

He's getting frustrated, tired of trying to communicate with her and it's fifty–fifty whether she responds.

Damn it, answer me, please. We need help.

Still nothing.

Emma hears Lance, but the kids need to figure out where Ryan is on their own. It's another weird decree she is obligated to follow so she remains silent.

Without any help or direction from Emma, Lance decides that Joey's option is better than no option at all.

"Let's go to the factory," he says as he visibly cringes.

All three boys are solemn, none of them looking forward to finding what awaits them.

CHAPTER 6

GOODBYE BEAR. I LOVE YOU

The road ahead of them is straight, straight and even, no hills, no bushes, no landmarks for miles. The orange hue of the sky and red dirt of the desert is surreal and holds nothing but bad, bad memories for the boys.

Reno is indifferent, but only because she still has not come to grips with her new reality. She's excited, scared, and right now miserable, wishing she brought a headband for her hair. There is now no doubt in her mind that the boys have been telling the truth, especially since their adventure in Sin City.

The heat from the black car with black interior is sweltering and puts everyone on edge. Jeremy swears that the milk he drank at home before leaving is now curdling in his stomach and turning into yogurt. Bear is on the floorboard between Lance's feet panting with his tongue lazily hanging out of his mouth.

"Is it always like this?" Reno asks.

"We don't know. This is all we remember. It must mean we're on the right road to the factory," Lance answers as he secretly shakes his canteen, confirming to himself that it's empty.

"Wait. What is that?" Lance is pointing off to the right side of the road at a gas station.

"Fuck, that can't be the same gas station. Please don't let it be," Jeremy squeaks out as he follows Lance's finger.

And then they see the sign, *Shell Gasoline ~ Diner*, and a smaller sign reads, *Owned and operated by Garland and Genevieve Parsons*.

"Shit, it is. I don't want to stop. Please don't stop," Jeremy says as he sinks down into his hot seat.

"Why? Maybe it has water or food," Reno replies.

The boys know it will have neither. The only thing that wicked place has is bad memories. Each of the boys remember it in their own way. Walking in with Charlie and seeing the three pretty girls behind the counter. At first they were excited, sure they were going to get lucky. In a way, they kind of did. The trio was eventually making out with the girls. For Joey, it was extra special. He was making out with Wendy, his crush from earlier in that purple apartment. And then all hell broke loose. Charlie changed the girls back into their true groupling selves and they started rotting right in front of them. Lance vividly remembers making out with his crush, Toni, and her rotting lip somehow ended up in his mouth, and he chewed on it before he realized what it was.

"I agree. I don't think that place has anything we can use in there," Lance says, twinging as he wipes his tongue with his hand. The tainted flavor of rotting meat is as prominent as the day it happened and is giving him a case of dry mouth. He looks down at Bear and has a change of heart. "Actually, maybe we do need to stop to see if there's water. Bear is dying down here."

"Hopefully there's a spigot on the outside. If not, who's going in? Not it!" Joey yells as he places his finger on the tip of his nose. The others automatically play along. Lance loses.

"Jo-Jo, you're the only one that's been in the kitchen area. Did you see a sink or anything?" Jeremy asks.

"I don't fucking know. I was passing second base rounding third before Wendy's fucking face rotted the fuck off."

"We're all going in and that's that," Reno demands.

Case closed.

They park in the back next to the kitchen entry. A rusted ten-yard green dumpster is guarded by two fifty-five-gallon drums used for old fry grease. The door is smudged and oily from years of faithful service, the screen door long gone. When Reno turns the engine off and swings open her door, all three boys look at each other, not saying a word, but understanding what the other is thinking. They're scared and don't want to go in. They reluctantly get out and immediately pull their knives.

"Who's going in first? It sure the fuck ain't me," Joey says as he moves behind Lance and Jeremy.

Lance takes the lead. He lost the game and throws open the door and yells, "Hello, anyone in there?"

All of them wait, quietly listening. Hearing nothing, Lance walks in knife forward like he's holding an épée preparing for a duel. The kitchen area is clear, no grouplings. He finds the dishwashing station and three stainless steel sinks, dirty dishes stacked in every available basin and counter teeter haphazardly waiting for a slight breeze to blow them over. He turns the handle to the faucet, and at first, there's nothing, and then the pipes clank to life as rusty water makes its way through clogged arteries. It explodes out of the small nozzle shooting red liquid everywhere.

"You have to give it a minute to clear up if it hasn't been used in a while; the pipes might be a little rusty," Joey offers the group.

"Thanks, Jo-Jo, but we know," Lance says out loud, but is thinking, *Fucking hurry up, my mouth is so dry I can drink a gallon of water right now.*

Eventually, the water clears and Lance shoves the dirty dishes onto the floor and sets Bear on the counter to drink.

At the same time, Reno hears a scratching noise outside and unwisely leaves the boys without telling them. As soon as she exits the building, she's face-to-face with two male grouplings that must have been part of a motorcycle club in their prior life. They have long hair, long beards, and are wearing matching denim cuts with red and yellow colors of the Norse fire giant sitting on the sun. They grab her and she starts screaming.

Bear hears her first and immediately leaps off the counter and runs out the door. The boys arrive just in time to see one of the grouplings grab Bear by the neck, choking him, and then drop him and kick him like a football with his big, black, pointed boot. Bear lets out a whimper and flies fifteen feet through the air, landing on his side, motionless.

Lance screams as he charges the groupling, plunging the hunting knife into its chest, the momentum taking both of them to the ground. Jeremy pulls Reno out of the arms of the other groupling and Joey stabs it multiple times in the shoulder and neck pushing it onto the hood of the GTO, blood spraying everywhere. Jeremy kicks it in the balls and it releases a high-pitched gurgling as it slides to the ground. All three boys turn their attention to the groupling that kicked Bear and begin circling it like sharks attacking wounded prey. They mercilessly kick it in the torso and head, their rage overwhelming them.

Joey drags the groupling to the concrete step at the entrance of the door and makes it bite the edge and screams, "Fuck you!"

He jumps and lands on the back of its head shattering its teeth and breaking its jaw. Lance and Jeremy cringe and turn away. Joey keeps kicking and stomping the groupling as they drag him away trying to calm him.

Lance remembers Bear and runs over to him, fearing the worst. Bear's already in Reno's arms. Reno is crying as she rubs his head, crying and rocking him.

"Is he alive? Is he going to be alright?" he asks, tears building and his body shaking as he looks his best friend over. Bear looks up with his puppy dog eyes and then lays his head back down on Reno's lap.

"He's hurt real bad, Lance, but I think he's going to survive," she says, wobbling as she stands. She walks toward the kitchen door and stops mid-step. "I can't go over there." She points to the groupling with the crushed face, blood and teeth splattered on the door and wall. She hands Bear to Lance; he steps over the groupling and takes Bear in for a drink of water.

Joey and Jeremy pull the other groupling out of the way so they don't run him over when they leave. Joey is the only one that does not look visibly shaken and he wants to make sure these two grouplings won't get up and attack again. He jabs each of them in the back of the neck with his knife looking for a reaction, neither respond, and Joey is satisfied they won't be getting up, but he knows they're grouplings so they will eventually come back to life and he doesn't want to be around when that happens.

"Lance, hurry the fuck up before these shitbags come back to life," Joey yells over his shoulder.

A couple of minutes later, Lance emerges with Bear from the kitchen, his eyes puffy and red. All four of them silently get into the car and Reno starts the engine. As Reno pulls away, she runs over a groupling's leg. The boys didn't move him far enough out of the way.

They were only driving for a few minutes when Reno slams on the brakes as she points toward the sky in front of them. "What the hell is that?"

Lance looks where she's pointing and sees four black dots in the orange sky coming toward them. He knows what they are, highwaymen, the big, black, featherless, vultures coming to take the two dead grouplings.

"Highwaymen, keep driving. I don't know if they will try to attack us," Lance answers.

Reno doesn't want to find out and guns the engine and the GTO launches down the road.

They drive for hours and Lance has Bear curled up in his lap.

Please God, don't let Bear die. He's a good dog, I love him so much. I promise I'll be better. I won't smoke or drink. I won't skip school anymore, please just let him live. He was trying to protect Reno. He's a good dog. He's my best friend, please God, please.

Lance is crying and doesn't care if the others can hear him now.

Bear's labored breathing is getting worse. His internal bleeding is slowly killing him and his broken ribs cause involuntary '*yips*' of pain as he draws air. Bear and Lance grew up together and their love is reciprocal. Bear is his best friend. Thinking about life without Bear, consumes every fiber in his body and Lance's tears flow freely down his face. Lance wishes he could rewind and start over from the beginning, the last day of school. He would stay home instead of trying to go to Larry's stupid party. If he stayed home, he would not have gone to the Thriftway Building Center and none of this would have happened.

The pain is too great for Bear to lift his head all the way, but he does his best to take one last look at his big brother. They lock eyes and Lance sees and feels the love Bear has for him. Once again, Lance wishes he could communicate with Bear the way he does with Emma.

Bear lays his head back down on Lance's lap, grateful that he will die in his arms. He shuts his eyes for the last time and his breathing ceases.

Lance knows that Bear just died but he doesn't want to believe it. He sits frozen, silent, wishing for Bear's little chest to rise again.

He leans down so his face is touching Bear's and begins crying uncontrollably.

The others remain silent, allowing Lance to have his last moment with Bear. All three of them are quietly crying. It hurts Reno knowing that Bear blindly rushed out of the kitchen to try and save her. She feels it's her fault. She's shaking so bad and the tears are so heavy that she has to pull over onto the side of this road.

Lance gets out of the car cradling Bear in his arms. He knows he has to bury Bear, but wishes he didn't have to do it here in this evil, forsaken hellhole. He finds a rock and starts digging a hole. The others join him and soon they have a small grave carved out of the red dirt. Lance gently places Bear in his new eternal home. He pulls Bear's favorite toy out of his backpack, a gnarled red and white rubber chew toy shaped like a bone.

No matter where Lance was in his house, Bear would show up with his bone and push it with his nose as close to Lance as he could for Lance to protect it and keep it safe from Bear's imaginary thieves.

He places the toy in between Bear's front legs close to his chest. They fill the hole and Lance says a prayer. All of them stand, silently reminiscing about their fondest memories with Bear. The kids make their way back to the car and silently get in. Lance is still standing by Bear's grave. He's having a hard time leaving him here in this evil place. He asks God to promise him that he will find him here in Sheol and take him to heaven. It hurts Lance that he has to leave him alone. He turns and gets in the car and sits with a distant look on his face. All of his friends feel sorry for Lance. They all know how much Bear means to him. With the funeral over, they continue their journey toward the factory.

Standing on the same marble steps he walked down after receiving his punishment at the hands of Delphine, Charlie smiles a wicked smile. He promised her on this step that he would return and make her pay, make her eat herself, and today is payday.

He convinced Erebus to let him have his revenge early. This time Charlie will have a marked advantage. The last time his powers were useless. Tonight he walks into the house of horrors rejuvenated, confident, and vengeful.

Inside, Delphine is punishing Miss Rebecca for spilling sweet tea all over the kitchen floor.

As soon as Charlie crosses the threshold, Delphine feels his presence and pauses. She has Rebecca's arm submerged to the elbow in a huge, boiling, forty-gallon commercial pot of mudbugs and fingers. Her plan was to keep Rebecca's arm in the boiling water until the flesh fell off, adding flavor to the meal. She pulls her arm out and stuffs a hand cloth into Rebecca's mouth to stifle her screams.

Delphine is having a dinner party and there are about forty guests in the dining hall anxiously awaiting their crawdads and fingers. They will have to wait just a little bit longer.

Charlie confidently walks into the house, passing the guests chatting amongst themselves, and into the kitchen. Rebecca is kneeling on the floor. She's holding her arm, her mouth stuffed so she can't speak, but Charlie can read the pain in her eyes. The flesh on her arm looks like someone poured hot wax on it and it's dripping onto the spotless kitchen floor, coming off in globs. Delphine is standing in the center of the kitchen, her hubris filling the elegant black party dress and sparkling like the expensive jewelry around her neck and fingers.

"Hello, Mr. Stratt. I've been expecting you, but to be honest, not this soon," she says as she nods at Rebecca to pick her pathetic, insolent self off the ground.

"Yes, well, I'm a man of my word, Delphine. Hello Miss Rebecca, I see you are hating your life right now." He nods toward Delphine's master chef.

She barely looks up and gives the slightest nod.

"Well, this is awkward; would you like to stay for dinner, Mr. Stratt?" Delphine asks.

"As a matter of fact, yes. What's on the menu tonight?"

"All of the mudbugs and corn you can eat," she says, leaving out the fingers that replaced the sausage.

"Hmm, sounds good, but I have a better idea. Tonight, your dinner guests in the other room and the prisoners you have locked away are going to dine on a big, fat, cow." He points his finger directly at Delphine, hatred, and fire burning in his eyes.

She does not know that Charlie's power works in her house. Her house is like a Wi-Fi dead spot, normally, but not today, and not for Charlie. She lets out an angry shriek as she rushes Charlie, expecting him to be the same feeble, broken man he was before. "I'm going to eat your brain and keep you alive so you can watch!"

"Thank you. I think I will do that to you," he says and flicks his hand, making the boiling pot fly across the room and collide into her midsection; her skin immediately turns red and blisters.

Her blood-curdling scream startles her dinner guests in the other room and Rebecca shrinks into the corner of the kitchen, whimpering, covering her eyes.

Delphine realizes the gravity of her situation, but she's stubborn. She's had her way for centuries in this house and she's not going to give up easily. Ignoring the pain, she crawls across the floor, slipping on the water, and grabs a large knife off the counter with the intent of carving out Charlie's eyeballs. He allows her to secure the blade and freezes her in her tracks so she can't move.

"Del, not going as expected, huh?" He smiles, calmly walking toward her and gives Rebecca a quick wink. He takes the knife out of Del's hand and wrinkles his nose as he looks at the blisters on her neck and arms. "I hope your guests will still want to partake in the Delphine special tonight."

He motions to Rebecca with his only arm and her iron collar falls from her neck.

"Miss Rebecca, will you please retrieve the monkey table I saw in the storeroom the last time I was here, please."

Rebecca, rubbing the scars on her neck says, "Mr. Stratt, what is a monkey table?"

"The table with the hole in the middle."

The monkey table is a wood table used to secure its victim's neck so the head is above and the body below the tabletop.

"Roll it out to the dining hall."

Charlie opens the serving door and motions for the four servants staged in the same spot they were last time in the dining hall to come into the kitchen as he walks out to address the dinner guests. "Ladies and gentlemen, if you do not want to end up on tonight's menu, I recommend you leave immediately."

The guests may not know what is happening, but they all heard the commotion in the kitchen and Delphine's screams. Anyone or anything that can make Delphine scream is not someone to mess with, they know. They frantically scramble to their feet and head toward the door, loudly questioning Charlie but not slowing as they make their way to the exit. It's a good thing because right now, Charlie is not in the mood. He returns to the kitchen as Rebecca and another servant are rolling the monkey table past Delphine.

She realizes what Charlie has in store for her. He is going to keep his promise of making her eat herself. She commands them to stop, to not listen to Charlie, or else. Her threats fall on deaf ears.

"You three, bring me the other prisoners, all of them, now," he states, staring a hole through Delphine. "How many of them are there?"

"Twenty-two, sir," the last servant says over his shoulder as he walks out.

"Delphine, follow me."

"Fuck you, release me now or you will be sorry. You can't do this. Erebus won't let you, you son of a bitch," she says still frozen by Charlie's spell.

Rebecca comes back into the kitchen and Charlie motions for her to take Delphine into the dining hall. Rebecca tries to pick her up, to move her, but she can't. The whole time Delphine unleashes a new round of threats and it takes everything Rebecca has in her to keep from laughing out loud. She's skeptical and reserved, but deep down she knows it's already too late. If Delphine ever recovers, she will unleash hell on all who wronged her.

Charlie walks back into the kitchen and grabs a handful of Delphine's hair and leads her out to the dining hall, Delphine cussing him the entire way.

The monkey table pulls apart to allow the victim's head to be positioned in the middle. The servant slides it closed and secures the brass hasp and a padlock. Delphine looks ridiculous with her head protruding out of the center of the table. The expensive diamond tiara looks so out of place now on her burned, pathetic head. The prisoners are herded into the dining hall. If they could show emotion, it would be classified as shock as they see their monstrous mistress pathetically pleading to be released, abandoning her threats.

Charlie spots Mr. Garrington in the middle of the pack, now missing his left leg along with his arm. When Charlie sees him, all he can think is what Delphine said to him after their last meal, about feasting on rump roast. Charlie calls him over.

"Mr. Garrington, do you remember me?"

"Of course, why are you back? I would never come back. Are you crazy?"

"I've been told that. I want you to sit with me at the table of honor. Will you join me?" He points to the small circular table.

"No," he says with fear in his eyes. He knows that Delphine is in a bad spot now, but what about later after Charlie is gone and Delphine is back in power?

Charlie reads the room and understands the hesitation and fright in all of the prisoners. He leaps onto the top of the large dining table and begins walking the length of it, exaggerating his hand movements for emphasis. The inflection in his voice plays his crowd like a seasoned motivational speaker.

"Listen, I understand all of you are frightened and do not understand what is going on. Please, everyone, take a seat."

The prisoners silently pick their seats, staring ahead.

"Erebus has granted me and all of you, the power to make Delphine pay. She cannot retaliate. She cannot hurt any of us ever again."

What Charlie is telling them is not entirely true. Erebus did grant Charlie the use of his powers in Delphine's house. The council did not say what would happen after he leaves and the fate of the prisoners never came up. They don't know that, and right now their blank stares are turning red with revenge, hunger replacing their fright.

Mr. Garrington sits at the small table joining Rebecca.

Before Charlie dismounts the table and takes his seat he says, "All, tonight we are having Delphine for dinner."

He ends his monologue with an animated bow. They respond with a modest, reserved clap, but not loud enough to drown out Delphine's shrill voice pleading for mercy.

Her eyes turn yellow and her pupils dilate into slender vertical black slits. "Do not do this! Anyone that takes part in this will pay dearly. You pieces of shit think you have it bad now, just wait. I will feed you your fucking hearts."

The room quiets and Charlie knows he has to win it back. He opens a small drawer just above his seat and pulls out three small brass hammers that resemble a rock hammer with a blunt end and an elongated chisel on the other.

These hammers will be used to crack Delphine's skull to gain access to her gray brain.

Charlie removes her tiara and sets it on Rebecca's head, Delphine's shrieks for her property to be returned.

Charlie uses the blunt end first and cracks her head with the hammer and she lets out a blood-curdling scream.

"I will feed you worms. You will eat worms!" Fat nightcrawlers flow out of her mouth and nose eliciting gasps from the dinner guests.

"It's an illusion! Hit her!" Charlie yells at Mr. Garrington and Rebecca as he takes another healthy swing.

They join him and Delphine begins spinning under the table, her head looks like a toy top above. They keep smashing her over and over, blood flowing down her head mixing with the worms, a red slime covering her face. Charlie stops to admire their work and takes a knife out of the drawer to cut the skin and hair away to expose the cracked skull beneath. As he removes chunks of skull, worms begin crawling out of her head.

It's a grotesque scene that would make the most avid horror movie junkie turn away.

He grabs a handful of worms and throws them on the floor exposing her brain. Rebecca begins dishing out portions on their plates, pulling stray worms out and discarding them.

"Del, I believe you should enjoy the first bite," Charlie says as he slaps her until she opens her eyes and regains consciousness. He forces a healthy bite down her throat, laughing, "Not so big and tough now, are you? And quit begging; it's beneath even you." He turns to his guests. "Rebecca, I think these brains need a little salt, don't you?"

Rebecca nods taking the slim silver salt shaker and shakes a healthy portion of the white spice onto their plates.

Unable to keep up the optical illusion the worms begin dissipating, signaling to the others that Del's power is weakening.

Delphine, in a drugged, euphoric state from her wounds, begins giggling and talking excitedly to the table. She is not aware of who she is or where she is, but most importantly, she does not realize her dreadful situation.

Charlie takes the tiara. "Del, you look so pretty tonight. Do you want to wear your tiara?" He holds it in front of her.

"Yes, I'm so beautiful. I look like a princess." She smiles, blood running down her face.

Charlie takes the tiara and places it on her cracked and jagged head. "You know what? I have an idea. You should eat your face. Doesn't that sound yummy? All of your dinner guests want to see you eat your nose, will you do that for them, Del?" He gestures to the big table, encouraging them to clap.

"Yes, I'm so thirsty and hungry, that sounds great. What is your name again?" she asks, licking her lips. "Who are you? You are so nice and handsome. You're very handsome," she says to Charlie with a little wink.

"I'm Mr. Stratt, we've been good friends for a long time," he says as he motions for Rebecca to release Delphine from the bondage of the monkey table.

The dining hall falls silent, the prisoners don't understand what is happening, but are intently watching what is playing out at the little table. Delphine is released and stands, clear white liquid mixing with the blood on her face.

Charlie takes her hand and pulls her close to him, and they begin a grotesque, slow ballroom dance toward the big table.

"Here my lady, please take the seat of honor," he says, helping her sit.

She giggles.

Charlie feels fully vindicated now and picks up a small stainless-steel paring knife and hands it to her.

"Do you know what sounds good? Cheek, so tender and the texture is to die for," he says, licking his lips.

Delphine nods in agreement and begins carving off a piece of her right cheek. She licks it and then pops it into her mouth, oohing and awing to herself the way someone would when eating a luxurious chocolate truffle.

Charlie stands and takes a modest bow and walks toward the door.

"Ladies and gentlemen, the buffet is now open," he says to the room, knowing when he leaves the prisoners will rip her apart and devour her.

Charlie never found out what happened after he left that night. The prisoners did feast and have their short-lived revenge. Like Charlie, Delphine is a general in Erebus's army and an important cog in their evil machine. Erebus resurrected her and restored her power and authority in full. The hell the prisoners lived prior to that night feels like a Disneyland vacation compared to now. Even if Charlie did know what was going to happen to the prisoners, he would not have cared or changed that night. That night was all about Charlie getting his revenge and now he has a clear mind and is laser-focused on the boys.

Amy walks through the slaughterhouse door and takes in her new Adamah surroundings. It's pitiful compared to what she is used to back in Chicago. She's out in the country with no sign of life anywhere other than a few birds singing in the trees. She wonders why Charlie would send her to this forsaken place. She was happy at the drug den. In fact, she prefers the homeless degenerates compared to this empty shithole. All she can think is Charlie is punishing her for something, but she does not know why. She's one of his best producers and she knows he likes how violent and sadistic she is when she turns the recruits. He did not offer an explanation. He just ordered her to this place with no further instruction. If he sent her, then it must be for a reason. But why didn't he send Ryan with her? They are a team.

Charlie has a plan for Amy. If things go bad between him and the kids and he needs some backup, he wants the most ruthless and obedient groupling in his army. She will do what he wants without question. The other reason Charlie wants her here is Ryan. If he has to bring Ryan, Amy will help keep him in check.

It's daytime and the sun is beating down on her. Something she's not used to in Chicago where she normally only enters the city at night. She cannot smell the fumes from automobiles, the rot of trash piled in the alleys, or the buzz of humans around her. She does not like it. Everything feels wrong.

She begins walking down the lonely dirt road close to the edge to take advantage of the shade of the trees. She wants to find new hunting grounds and she knows it's not here. She will have to walk for nearly an hour before she reaches I-84, passing a couple of farmhouses along the way. She finally sees a sign, a huge semi-truck hoisted up in the air and on the side of the trailer it reads *Baker Truck Corral*. She found a truck stop and she's recruited from them before. Her parched lips crack a smile and she hastens her pace toward it.

She doesn't even make it ten feet into the parking lot when she hears someone whistle. The catcall is coming from a brown and white Peterbilt cab-over idling in the lot. It's a young truck driver standing in the shade of the semi. He's a good-looking man wearing brown boots, blue jeans, and a red baseball cap. He's noticeably missing his shirt and his six-pack abs are glistening from sweat. Amy immediately turns toward him and she can feel his eyes undressing her with every step.

"Damn missy, you're way too pretty to be walking around this dump alone. You with anybody?" he asks as he reaches into his cab and pulls out a white T-shirt. He uses it to wipe the sweat from his body and then tosses it back inside. He notices she doesn't answer him but keeps walking toward his truck. He thinks she must be a lot lizard, a prostitute. Most women from around here don't look as pretty as her and her clothes sure ain't country.

When she reaches the truck, she slides next to him to share the shade. He gets a good look at her and winks. She's short and beautiful. Her sweat has inadvertently turned her white blouse see-through and he has a hard time not staring at her black bra underneath. If a strong wind comes up it will blow her short miniskirt up and he will get another free peek. He now wishes for wind.

"I'm Amy, what's your name?" she asks, wiping sweat from her forehead.

He smiles. "Everyone calls me hot Carl." He pulls the T-shirt back out and offers it to her.

She curls her nose. She'll be damned if she uses his truck-driver sweaty shirt.

"You want to go inside and get a cold ice tea? My treat," he asks her. "Or, I have some cold water and some beers inside."

He points to his cab and hopes she declines the offer to go into the truck stop. He really doesn't want anyone else seeing her with him. Not because he's married or embarrassed she might be a lot lizard, but for another reason.

"I'll take a beer. Does your truck have A/C?" she asks, tracing a bead of sweat with her finger as it rolls down her neck between her cleavage.

"Hell yeah, jump in," Hot Carl says with a twinkle in his ice-blue eyes.

After about thirty minutes and three cans of beer, they decide to go to Amy's place so they can make some noise without the worry of nosy neighbors hearing them. They drive until they are on a deserted road and then it happens.

Amy is out of her element and does not react quickly enough to the syringe stabbed into her neck. Carl has injected her with a dose of succinylcholine, SUX for short. A drug that causes muscular paralysis and keeps the victim wide awake.

Hot Carl pulls over, the slaughterhouse in view ahead of him. He reaches over and pinches Amy's nipple hard, and cracks a shit-eating grin. She does not react, but he knows she is awake. She cannot breathe on her own and he knows she will expire soon. He verbally belittles her while having his way.

What Amy did not know is she met her human match—a sadistic misogynist that would make even Charlie proud. His hatred of women stems back to his childhood and his dad's second wife.

He opens the door and pushes Amy out of the cab. She dies in Adamah and maybe her death is fitting after all that she has done alive and as a groupling.

CHAPTER 7

RYAN, IT'S ME!

Ominous, dark, and haunting, the abandoned factory begins to come into view ahead of them. Lance automatically glances up at the orange sky to see if it's filled with black vultures. It's not, and they at least have that on their side. The closer they get, the more anxious the boys become.

The factory is where it all happened—where the kids world almost ceased to exist.

They really, really don't want to go in there. Lance can't help think that there's got to be another way, another way to save Ryan without going into that fucking hell hole.

Jeremy is visibly shaking in the back seat and his mind has basically shut down. The impending doom is too much for his fragile mental state and his stomach agrees as its goaded into involuntary spasms.

Lance notices that there are no grouplings littering the landscape and the road is not bubbled and cracked with massive sinkholes.

He remembers their first trip. The sky was black with highwaymen and thousands of grouplings were migrating toward the factory. Charlie ordered Joey to run them over and to quit swerving to avoid them. And then the earth began rolling, cracking, and breaking, swallowing huge chunks of road.

None of that is present now. It's as if that never happened, but it does nothing to ease Lance or the other boys' minds.

They arrive and the red Camaro is parked right where they left it next to the retaining wall. It's now covered in a thick layer of red dust. Reno parks next to it, not knowing its significance, and none of the boys offer to tell her that this is the car they rode in with Charlie.

As they exit the car, Joey hears his specter who he has now named, Harpy. "Take them to the room."

Joey knows what room he's talking about. It's the room where all of it happened; the rift opening, Charlie turning into a spinning glob of who-the-fuck knows-what, and it's where the phoenixes helped Lance defeat Charlie. Joey doesn't want to go into the room and he knows for damn sure Lance and Jeremy don't want to.

"No," he blurts out to Harpy.

To frighten Joey, Harpy reveals itself and it's hideous—a large, skinny, gray, bald, aberration of evil. Its eyes are the size of a fist, black with no pupils. Its body is wiry and defined, with cuts and scars covering nearly every inch. But it's the mouth that really scares Joey. Its mouth runs from ear to ear, except it has no ears, and the inside is black with a small pink tongue like a fish. It has two rows of uneven, long, sharp feline teeth that are yellowed and black, some of them broken and jagged.

"I said take them to the room!" Harpy thunders at Joey, sending him toppling back into the Camaro.

The other kids stare at Joey, confused, wondering if he tripped on something. Joey is the only one that can see and hear his new friend.

"You okay, Jo-Jo, you clumsy twat?" Jeremy chides in a joking tone.

"Yeah, douchebag. I slipped," Joey says as he slaps the rear end of the Camaro and moves to the door and wipes the dust from the window.

All three boys look inside. None of them brave enough to even try and open the door. The inside looks just as they remembered, bad.

As Lance relives the moment when he handed Jeremy his talisman, right before he jumped out of the car killing himself, Emma finally communicates with him. Emma and Harpy are unaware that the other exists, communicating with their respective boys. They can't see or feel the other's presence.

"Lance, do not go into the factory. Ryan is not there," Emma says, warning him that Charlie has laid a trap.

"Thank God. We really didn't want to go in there," Lance says quietly as he pulls Joey and Jeremy away from the car. They offer no resistance. In fact, they are glad.

"Where is he then?" he asks as he motions for everyone to get into the GTO so they can make a hasty escape.

Harpy is furious that they are back in the car and not going into the factory. They must go into the factory.

It flashes again showing Joey its anger. "Go into the factory, all of you now, or your friends will die." It can't physically hurt them, but it can try to scare Joey into compliance. "Now!" Its snarled face twists and its eyes bulge, its veins pulsing and bursting on its head and neck.

Joey knows they are in trouble if they don't act fast and his fear succumbs him to where he can't think straight. He pulls his knife out of his pocket, expecting the worst is about to happen. Harpy grins and points to the sky. Joey follows Harpy's hand and can see hundreds of black dots speckling the sky. It's the highwaymen. The other kids have not seen them yet. They must act fast.

"Fuck! The highwaymen are coming!" Joey screams, pointing. As soon as the other kids see them, they join his screams. Reno starts the GTO and speeds away from the factory.

Jeremy yells, "What about Ryan? Isn't he in the factory? We need to save him!"

"No, he's not in there. The factory is a trap. We should've never come," Lance answers, looking back at Joey.

Now Lance knows Joey set them up, convinced them to come to the factory, but why? Maybe if they survive, he will ask him. He now has no doubt in his mind that Joey is working against them, either on purpose or inadvertently. He hopes for the latter.

The highwaymen are close now, close enough that Reno can clearly see one of their heads, and it scares the shit out of her. She screams just as the vulture slams into the back of the car, testing the shocks, forcing the car to bounce. The vulture is flopping on the road behind them, its mouth gaped open, neck twisted, and its left-wing bent and twisted behind its body.

Jeremy is sure they will all die, never get out of this wicked place alive. He decides there is no chance of escape so he leans forward and puts his arms over his head, waiting for the final death blow he knows is coming.

More and more vultures smash into the car, breaking the windows and leaving huge dents in the roof and trunk. So far, they have been lucky. There's no damage to the engine or tires; the car is still operational.

"What do we do? Where do we go? If there was ever a time to help, now is the time," Lance asks Emma, half expecting a reply.

"Keep driving. There is a building up ahead. It's a portal and I believe it will lead to Ryan," Emma answers.

"Keep driving, Reno. There's a building. We want to get to that building," Lance says.

Reno is pushing the speed past the century mark and the car is humming along with more to give, other than a slight wobble it is handling fine. She bobs and weaves across the road minimizing the accuracy of the highwaymen. Many of them end up on the road behind them, crumpled and flopping in pain. The kids are now optimistic that they are going to make it to the new building in part due to Reno's driving. They have to make it, whatever and wherever the building is.

⸻

Charlie has just left Delphine's house when he has a vision and sees the GTO driving away from the factory. He is incensed that Joey's specter failed. He commands more highwaymen and grouplings toward the kids. He will throw everything he has at them. He knows where they are going now: the movie theater.

⸻

They come screaming in hot and Reno does her best to regain control of the GTO as the passenger side slams into the brick building, pinning the passenger door closed. They are at the movie theater, a yellow, 1960s art deco building with large arches outlining, *Copeland Theater*. The marquee below reads, "Alfred Hitchcock's, Psych-." The "o" is long gone.

All four of them get out of the vehicle on the driver's side, highwaymen still bombarding them with their kamikaze suicide dives, smashing into the GTO, the building, and street, withering and letting out shrieks of pain so loud it sounds like a loudspeaker next to their grotesque beak–snouts. The kids run past the boarded-up ticket booth and through the ornate glass double doors leading to the lobby.

Once inside, they frantically look around for a safe place. The red and yellow carpet below their feet is frayed and ripped. Joey runs toward the auditorium to the right while the other three turns left leading to a set of stairs.

"Joey, what are you doing? Don't go in there. Follow us!" Reno screams as she reaches the bottom of the stairwell. Joey stops dead in his tracks, feet away from the auditorium doors and swivels pointing himself in their direction and runs just as the doors slam open and grouplings come pouring out, chasing after him.

"Shit, shit, help!" Joey yells, running as fast as he can, past the concession stand toward the stairs. At least twenty grouplings are chasing him. And they're fast.

Lance reaches the top of the stairs and before he grabs the door handle he says a very quick prayer, "Please let the door be unlocked."

It's locked.

"Shit no!" he screams, kicking the door. Now all four of them are trapped in the little stairwell. Jeremy pushes the others out of the way and shoulder checks the door as hard as he can. He hits it with so much force he falls back and all of them tumble down the stairs. They are trapped and Charlie's grouplings are now approaching the bottom getting ready to make their way up.

"Emma, please help us," Lance says out loud, now that his prayer to God didn't work.

"Lance, you can open the door; you can stop the undead; you must believe in yourself," she replies.

"How, how the hell can I stop them? There're too many." He's hopeless and upset that Emma has left them for as good as dead.

"You have the power Lance, use it."

Reno is toward the bottom of the stairwell and one of the grouplings grabs her leg and begins pulling her into the pack. If Lance doesn't act fast, she is dead.

"STOP!" he screams from the top of the stairs, his voice echoing through the building. He's pointing at the groupling holding Reno and flicks his hand shooing it away. The groupling flies backward and smashes into the others, dropping all of them like pins in a bowling alley.

Holy shit, did I do that? he thinks as the grouplings clamor to their feet.

The other three kids are staring at him like he's a freak. Lance feels a sudden hot, searing pain in his chest and looks down, the talisman glowing blue hot is melting into his chest and disappears, only the faintest glow just under his skin remains. Lance feels empowered.

This is what Emma was talking about all this time. Lance finally understands. The talisman is more than just a rock. Emma is more than just a guardian angel. All of it, all this time, it has been molding Lance; his power grows stronger and stronger each day.

It's weird, but now he knows what he can do, how to use his powers. It's as if he's had them all this time and he's a practiced tactician.

Charlie gets a sharp shooting pain in his head when Lance throws the groupling. He knows that if he cannot stop him now, then he may never be able to stop him. He still needs both boys. Lance and Jeremy's blood are needed to intertwine Adamah and Sheol. The red liquid of their ancestors that holds the bewitched power to merge the worlds courses through them. He was so focused on Delphine and getting his revenge that he lost sight of the boys and Lance has been growing more and more powerful each day. He underestimated Lance, and he is furious that he allowed himself not to see what was happening. Charlie begins thrashing and ripping limbs off the grouplings around him, fire shooting out of his eyes and lightning out of his hands, screaming so loud he bursts the grouplings' eardrums. He leaves behind a tangled mess of body parts and blood as he disappears. He is going to the movie theater to end this once and for all with his bait in tow.

Ryan, in Chicago, has just crossed the threshold, back from another night of successful recruiting, holding the hand of his most recent victim when he suddenly feels a shock. It's like grabbing a live electrical wire. There is a brilliant red streak and the room explodes into an array of embers. He shrieks as he disintegrates from the drug den and reappears next to Charlie in the projector room of the movie theater, the recruit's dismembered hand still in his.

Charlie and Ryan can hear the commotion just outside the door. Charlie knows the kids are in the stairwell, but Ryan does not know what is going on.

He can't comprehend in his current state. He has no idea his friends are risking everything to save him.

To be cautious, Charlie flashes his hand across his own mouth and invisible fingers sew Ryan's lips shut. He squeals but cannot speak.

Charlie has not forgotten Harpy's colossal failure. He gestures at the door and it passes through like Casper the ghost and slams against the back wall next to Ryan. Ryan gives it a disinterested look, but it has Charlie's full attention. Charlie glides over to it. The room has a sinister, dark feel, and Charlie's eyes are black and growing. He is morphing into his true self, a monstrous, evil being, leaving his human form behind. He reaches his arm out and Harpy smashes into his twisted claws. Charlie opens his mouth, his jaw unhinges and sucks Harpy back into him, turning into a black mist as it disappears down his throat.

The kids on the other side of the door have no idea what is going on inside. They have no idea that only a door separates them from Charlie and Ryan.

Lance's confidence is building and he believes he has a chance to defeat the grouplings. He pushes the other kids behind him and becomes the barrier between his friends and the enemy. His mind is laser-focused and he raises both hands, arms extended out in front of him toward the grouplings. He makes fists with both hands, his right leg extended behind him for balance, and the stairs the grouplings are gathered on explode and crumble away. The grouplings fall, unable to advance.

"Fuck you! You're not going to get us, you sons a bitches," Lance yells as a small, vibrant ball of blue flames spin just above his open hands. The ball builds and grows until it's the size of a bowling ball and he flicks it toward the grouplings. On impact, it bursts and the stairwell fills with flames and smoke. When it clears, the grouplings are gone, black striations mark the ground and remaining walls. Lance looks down at his hands, not able to conceptualize what just happened. His friends look at him with shock and awe. They know that more grouplings will be coming for them so they need to get the door open.

"Lance, shoot that shit out of your hands again and open this damn door." Joey kicks the door looking back at Lance.

"How did you do that?" Reno asks, grabbing Lance's wrists and turning his hands up. Lance's palms are black and burnt, pink skin showing underneath. "Shit are you alright? Are your hands hurt?"

Lance rubs his hands on his jeans and looks at them in disbelief; burnt skin rubs off on his jeans. He lies to Reno. "No, I don't feel a thing."

His hands feel like they look, third-degree burns, and it hurts like hell, but he knows that if they are to survive, he will be the one to save them. He ignores the pain as he turns his attention to the door at the top of the stairs. He doesn't even really know why they need to get into the room. Maybe, it's not even the right door, but right now it's the kids' only option. Jeremy and Joey push up against the wall and slide behind Reno and Lance, giving Lance room to work.

"What do you think? You going to burn it down?" Jeremy asks as he keeps looking over his shoulder to make sure grouplings aren't reappearing at the bottom.

Lance doesn't want anything to do with fire if he can help it right now. He pulls his backpack off his shoulder and pulls a flathead screwdriver out and rams it in between the door and jamb. He pushes as hard as he can and feels it give a little, but it's not enough to spring the door. Joey sees what he's doing and stages himself next to Lance and nods. Lance does it again and Joey kicks the door as hard as he can just under the doorknob. The door almost cooperates, both boys nod at each other and do it one more time. This time, the door flies open and Joey loses his balance and stumbles into the room. When he looks up, he's staring straight into the dead eyes of his old friend Charlie.

Charlie snickers to himself knowing that he now has the boys.

Lance is still standing at the door and is the first one to spot Ryan in the back of the room; he says, "Ryan, it's me!"

CHAPTER 8

IF YOU DIE IN ADAMAH

ance quickly surveys the room, his eyes bouncing from the projector in the center to the rows and rows of movie reels that are all neatly stacked and labeled, and his gaze finally settles on Charlie's black, soulless eyes. Their eyes lock and like schoolyard kids, both refuse to be the first to blink and look away...to show weakness. There's a thick tension in the room weighing like a coda to their violent relationship.

Charlie can sense it's different this time. Lance has confidence and a new found power, a blue aura surrounds him. Charlie will not underestimate him again. Last time, it was Charlie's hubris that caused him to fail. This time he has Ryan as his ace card, and he has what he believes is a joker up his sleeve. He summons that joker.

"Joey, come over here to me." Charlie waves his mangled claw at him, his abhorrent face grinning the best it can as black blood pulses through his veins on the surface of his mangled head. His large, black, crow eyes are now vehemently staring a hole through Joey's soul.

Lance turns toward Joey and sees, or feels, that Joey is bewitched; Charlie's hypnotic grip is firmly wrapped around Joey's neck, strangling his free will. Lance reaches for Joey and the room explodes in a black brilliant light. Its rays seize their minds and all of the kids drop to their knees, hands clasped over their ears, screaming.

Joey is powerless to disobey and moves next to Ryan. Now Charlie controls two of Lance's friends. Lance opens his mouth, releasing a high-pitched, piercing scream that breaks Charlie's mind-bending light show and the room returns to the dull yellow of the single lightbulb.

Charlie knows the task at hand will not be easy. He has to get Lance and Jeremy back to the epicenter to finish what he started. He needs to amalgamate their blood to unlock the portal between Adamah and Sheol, releasing Erebus for good. He knows simply commanding the kids to follow him like before will not work. He will need to be diabolical and if anyone is diabolical, it's Charlie. He commands Joey to kill the new girl, knowing that Lance will be torn between his friend and the girl.

Joey's eyes fade to black and he pulls his knife out of his pocket and begins moving toward Lance and Reno. Under Charlie's command, he does not know what he is doing.

Lance knows it. Right now to Lance, Joey is evil and he will do what he needs to do to protect Reno, no matter how bad emotionally it hurts.

"Joey, please stop! Don't do this!" he yells as he backs up, his arm out to protect Reno. Reno screams. She doesn't know what is happening. She's so confused.

"It's not Joey. He's being controlled by Charlie. Don't trust him. He will hurt you," Lance quickly explains to her.

"Joey, what are you doing? Stop. It's me Reno," she says, now more frightened than ever. Up to this point, she has battled the undead and large black vultures, but now a friend, is trying to kill her. It's surreal. She can't escape. The stairs are demolished and there might be more grouplings down there. She's frozen, fear and confusion paralyzing her.

Lance puts his hand up as a warning to Joey that he will use his powers on him if he needs to, to save Reno. Joey ignores the warning and continues moving forward. Charlie's demonic figure performs a little dance to imitate a puppet on strings. He laughs out loud knowing Lance will have to choose who to save.

Joey lunges and Lance sidesteps him and strikes him in the back of the head with his backpack, sending him stumbling to the ground. Joey grunts and looks up, his black eyes blazing with hatred. He stabs himself in the stomach to show Lance nothing can hurt him.

Both Lance and Reno scream, but Lance knows that that will not stop Joey. Right now, Joey's mind is a black hole void of feelings or emotions, but past the black hole in the back recesses where Charlie does not have access, there is a small flicker of hope, faint but present.

How can Lance stop him without destroying him? Right now it doesn't look like that will be an option. Lance is pleading with him to remember that they are friends.

Nothing is registering. Joey stands and continues his march toward Reno, slamming his hand against his side spreading the blood with each strike.

Lance has no choice. He has to destroy Joey to save Reno. It's tearing him apart inside.

He's been friends with Joey for years. Joey let him stay with him for more than a week when his mom brought home a brutal asshole that would strike him with metal clothes hangers back when he was eleven.

But there's something intrinsic in Lance that will make him choose saving a female over a male. Maybe it's all the years of watching the low-life scum that calls themselves men hit his mom or perhaps it's something deeper, something in his genes. It could be the reason Emma is with him. Maybe he's just a good person. It saddens him, and now he's beginning to feel hopeless when Emma appears.

"Lance, the only way you can save yourself and your friends is to get Charlie to follow you to Adamah; he has limited power there."

"How, how Emma? I don't know how to get out of here," Lance says to her as he sizes up Joey to figure out his next move.

"You need to get him to follow you, run now!"

Lance grabs Reno's hand and they run down the demolished stairs. Leaping at the bottom to avoid the gaping hole of missing steps, they hit the floor and roll. Lance's backpack flies past them. It settles just out of reach. He looks up and scrambles toward his bag when he sees the grouplings closing in on them. He turns toward the stairs in time to see Joey leap toward him. His knife leading the way. Lance raises his hands emitting a blue glow. Joey freezes mid-air and crashes back up the stairs, banging into the walls. Lance turns his attention back to the grouplings. He knows he has to hurry. His hands are burning. He doesn't know if he can use his powers much longer if at all. The burns are trailing up his arms to his elbows and he can feel his blood boiling in his veins, and now there's a pressure in his head. It feels like the worst headache he has ever had, even worse than the time he cracked his head on the cement during a dark slide on a handrail that went terribly wrong. He scrambles to his feet and grabs Reno. They look for a way to escape. Ryan, hunched over, emerges, floating down the stairs. Charlie glides behind him holding an invisible leash walking his comatose dog.

"Lance! Isn't he the reason you're here? Don't you want to save him?" Charlie flicks Ryan who flies up and smashes into the oval roof and then lands hard on the ground letting out an "ooff" and lies motionless on the floor.

A spark of anger flashes in Lance's eyes. He forgets the pain in his head and hands. He launches toward Charlie. In the same instant, black lightning shoots from Charlie's hands. Lance is airborne when the lightning smashes into his chest. He flies hard into the wall.

They've forgotten Jeremy. But he's managed to get down to the lobby. He's next to Reno. The scene is chaos. Bodies are strewn everywhere. Charlie stands at the bottom of the stairs. Grouplings edge toward the kids.

A sense of hopelessness engulfs Lance. There's no possible way to escape.

Charlie is too strong and he's played a perfect game of chess, getting ready to checkmate Lance and his friends.

That flicker of hope, humanity, in the back of Joey's mind finally breaks free. Joey has been through so much and a weak mind would have succumbed long ago, murdering his friend Ryan, murdering Carter, the specter manipulating him, and of course Charlie and his hold on him. The forces of good have released him from the hold of the darkness, like sunlight eviscerating the mold. He can think clearly, and he knows he has to help save his friends.

"Fuck you!" he screams as he propels himself from the top of the stairs toward Charlie's back. His knife once again leads the way. Charlie turns his attention away from Lance to deal with Joey. But it's just enough time for Lance to react. He scrambles to where his friends are gathered. With all of his will and the little power left in his scrawny body, he makes a portal appears. He actually made a portal! He's stunned and when Charlie turns back around, he's equally stunned. Not knowing how long he can keep it open, Lance begins pushing his friends through. He takes one last look toward the stairs for Joey and not seeing any sign of him, he steps through the portal and disappears.

Charlie is furious. The lobby explodes and groupling body parts fly everywhere, coating the walls and floor with blood and chunks of flesh and bone. Charlie knows Erebus will not allow him to fail again, and if he does, he will spend an eternity in the house of horrors with whoever the new warden is that replaced Delphine.

Charlie is not aware Delphine is back, and if she gets her hands on Charlie again...

The kids are back in Adamah, back at the slaughterhouse, the cheerful pink pig winking at them as they lay sprawled out on the ground below.

Lance scrambles to his feet and begins taking a count of who is there: Reno, Jeremy, Ryan. Thank God, Ryan made it, but then Lance remembers Joey and begins looking for him and calling Joey's name. A feeling of doom, failure, overcomes him. He traded Ryan for Joey so he really didn't accomplish anything. He still failed. He flops down on his back, looking up at the bright sun, knowing that he could not save Joey. His hands and arms are burning and he shifts his attention to them. They are red and blistered.

He thinks, *That's going to leave a scar*.

He's tired, so tired, and so are the others. They lay next to him, all of them wanting to go to sleep. Maybe if they sleep and wake up, none of this will have really happened.

In Sheol, Charlie regains his composure. He's not going to let a snot-nosed kid bring him down again. He grabs Joey by the throat with the intention of pulling him apart limb by limb when he has a thought. He still has Ryan. Ryan is a groupling so Charlie has total control of him in Sheol or Adamah. He can make Ryan bring

Lance and Jeremy back. Make him convince them that Joey can still be saved. Lance won't let Joey die. He came back to save Ryan. He'll do the same for Joey.

Charlie is unaware that when Ryan passed through Lance's portal and not one of Charlie's, he regained his human self, mind and all. Ryan is essentially one of the boys again.

Ryan feels a slight tingle in his head. Laying there in the dead grass and dirt, he doesn't know what is causing it, but it's as if something, or someone, is calling to him. It's Charlie ordering him to bring the other two boys back to Sheol. He shakes his head and thinks he must be dehydrated and closes his eyes again. The sun feels so good on his face and for some reason he feels cheerful. That's the best way to explain it. He falls back to sleep, exhausted.

Charlie can't feel the connection. He doesn't know why, but he can't control Ryan. He decides on another plan: Joey. He's going to send Joey into Adamah to bring the two boys back, through his portal, not theirs.

Like a wisp of black smoke, he enters Joey's mind and begins wrecking his brain, his thoughts, his emotions, a pinball bouncing around out of control wiping the old Joey from existence until he's nothing more than a shell, a body with no human connection, no memory. This is unchartered territory for Charlie. He has never traveled this far inside anyone, never this intense, but he has to make sure whatever caused Joey to disobey doesn't come back, especially in Adamah. When he is done, Joey is a trembling mass, his black eyes dead, even deader than Charlie's. Charlie is convinced that he's totally destroyed the old Joey and now sets about putting his plan into action.

Joey steps over the threshold and exits the door of the slaughter-house. He sees the four figures sprawled out in the dirt and knows that is his target. He can't think for himself. He has no feelings.

Joey is doing what Charlie programmed him for, bringing Lance and Jeremy back. As he walks toward them, he steps on some twigs and all of the kids immediately sit up, alert, all of them except Ryan, who is still in a deep sleep. Reno is the first to notice it's Joey and she springs to her feet with a look of relief on her face.

"Joey! We thought we lost you forever! Thank God, you're okay. How did you get away?"

Joey does not answer her, doesn't even acknowledge her. His big black eyes are staring into space. Lance is the first to notice something is wrong. He grabs Reno by the arm to keep her from going forward.

"It's not Joey. It is, but it's not really him," he says pointing at Joey's eyes, a feeling of dismay flooding his mind. Reno sees it and stops in her tracks.

Like a tape recording, Joey begins spurting out his pre-determined lines.

"Lance and Jeremy, you have to follow me back. I will die if you don't save me," he says in a monotone voice.

Jeremy wakes up. "What the fuck is wrong with him?" he whispers to Lance, loud enough for Reno to hear but not Joey.

"I'm not sure. It's some kind of trick Charlie has to lead us back to Sheol," Lance says.

"What are we going to do? Follow him?" Reno asks them both.

"No, not you. He doesn't want you. He wants Jeremy and me. It's our blood he needs."

Lance is trying to figure out his next move. He knows Emma said that they have to get Charlie to cross the threshold into Adamah, but Charlie is too smart. He never crosses over. If he crosses over, his powers are limited and if he dies here he's dead, and he knows it.

Lance has a plan. It's a stupid plan, but it's the only one he believes will work. He has to cross back into Sheol, alone, and drag Charlie through *his* portal back to Adamah. If he goes alone, he doesn't have to worry about anyone else. It will be him against Charlie, mano-a-mano. Lance hopes that he's up to it. He feels drained, tired. He wishes he had about seventy-two hours to just sleep and regain his energy, but he knows that is not an option. Charlie won't wait.

"I have a plan, but I need all of you to listen to me. Don't question me. This is the only way," he says half-heartedly, refusing to look any of them in the eyes, which doesn't give Reno or Jeremy a vote of confidence.

"What is it? What are you going to do?" Jeremy asks, with Reno nodding in agreement.

"I have to go back to Sheol. Alone. It's the only way. I need you two to stay here and make sure Joey doesn't try to follow—"

"Fuck that, if you go, I go," Jeremy interrupts.

Lance knows he doesn't have the time to explain it to them, and even if he did, they would never agree to it.

He summons his energy and wishes they would sleep. They all slide to the ground, Joey included, and go into a deep sleep.

Wow, this is crazy, he thinks. *Who knew I had this kind of power here, too?*

He doesn't know how long it will last so he has to hurry. He closes his eyes and when he opens them, a blue portal shimmers in front of him. The sun's rays distort it and it reminds him of a rock thrown into a lazy lake, the ripples reverberate floating in the air. He says a quick prayer and steps through.

"Where is Jeremy?" Charlie asks as Lance appears out of thin air in front of him standing on the red and yellow carpet.

"I left him in Adamah. If you want him, you will have to go there and bring him back yourself, you piece of shit," Lance replies with confidence in his voice, but inside his mind is screaming with terror.

Charlie laughs a wicked, evil laugh and says, "He will follow when you don't return. He will follow."

Lance knows that he must act fast. He is keeping his portal open just behind Charlie and every second that passes his energy is draining like a flashlight left on. He will get weaker and slower with every passing moment. He has to decide if he wants to use his power or just rush Charlie and hope they both tumble into the portal. If he uses his power, Charlie will counter and Lance doesn't think he's strong enough to overpower him. He decides to rush him and use a good old-fashioned tackle.

During his brief, very brief, stint on the football team, the coaches told them to focus on the runner's waist, his head and arms can juke you and you will end up grabbing air, but the hips don't lie. Once you make contact, slide your head to the side and wrap-up with your arms, and drive the runner backward with your legs.

Lance decides it's now or never, and lets out a war cry and charges Charlie. He wraps his arms around his waist and with his legs churning, he pushes Charlie backward. They both topple into the portal.

Charlie is confused and refuses to believe he was just tricked by a kid, but here he is staring up at the sun bleeding through Lance's disheveled hair.

He was brought through Lance's portal, rendering his powers useless.

Fear consumes him and he is afraid, a feeling he's not used to in his world, Sheol.

He scrambles to his feet. Lance is still on the ground too weak to move. Jeremy, Reno, Ryan, and Joey are staring in disbelief, feet away from him.

Charlie looks around for Amy. She should be here waiting for him. He can't feel her presence and it scares him. She is his backup plan, the extra muscle he needs to destroy these snot-nosed kids. He calls for her in his head, and then out loud. Nothing. He does not know what happened to her, but he knows he can't count on her now.

"Joey, kill these motherfuckers!" Charlie commands.

Joey looks at the kids, turns and begins aggressively moving toward Charlie.

Scared, Charlie yells for him to get away. As he backs up, he turns and realizes his portal is just feet behind him at the slaughter-house door. He is suddenly confident and cocky, knowing he has an escape. Charlie swears he will have his revenge and the kids will pay dearly as he turns to run to his portal.

Lance musters all of the power he has left in his body and Charlie freezes, unable to move any further. Joey lunges at him with his knife in hand and stabs it deep into Charlie's chest.

Charlie lets out a painful scream as he clutches at his chest, feeling for the first time in a long time, his hot, red blood leave his human body. It feels different than what he experienced in Sheol, in Delphine's house.

He knows he's been beaten again by a little boy, but this time it is forever unless he can make it to his portal before his life expires.

He scrambles to his feet and begins running toward the door, stumbling and tripping over his own legs. Lance has no more energy and is powerless to stop him.

Jeremy sees his opportunity to contribute and breaks out in a run past Joey and leaps, lassoing Charlie around the neck and drags him down to the ground once again. This time Joey, Reno, and Ryan, pile on top of him holding him down. Joey is at the bottom and is thrusting his knife in and out of Charlie's neck and face, blood soaking all of the kids. They lay on top of him until they are sure he is dead-dead, and then they rise. No one says a word. None of them feel good about what they have done, with the exception of Joey, who inside his head is giving himself high-fives.

"Is it over, did we actually do it?" Reno asks, looking at all of the blood splattered on her arms and shirt.

"Yes, he is gone for good. Kind of unceremoniously, but still gone," Jeremy says.

Lance regains consciousness and sees his friends are a bloody mess and fear instantly consumes him. Then he sees Charlie's lifeless body and realizes that they have done it. He is still weak and his arms and head are killing him, but he lets out a forced smile and then covers his head so the others don't see the tears.

Images of Bear arrest his mind and Lance is sorrowful. He lost his best friend and he sobs quietly into his arms. He is happy Ryan is back with them. He is happy Charlie will never hunt them again. But he is so sad that he lost Bear.

The kids take a few minutes to rest and reflect on what they have just done.

They saved the world and no one will ever know or believe them. That's alright though. At least they have each other, a clandestine group of kids turned superheroes.

They turn their attention to Charlie's dead body and must decide what to do with it. Their first instinct is to shove the bloody blob back into Sheol where it won't curse the ground in Adamah.

Reno is the first one to state the obvious. "If we put this piece of shit back in Sheol, will he come back to life?"

The kids don't know, but they don't want to find out. They unanimously vote that idea down.

"Let's burn his body like they do on TV to make sure it can't come back," Joey offers, and then he has another idea. "But first we need to cut its head off, seen that in the movies too." He beams, proud that he's thought of everything.

"Dude, we are not going to burn its body or cut its head off," Jeremy says.

"Why not? I'll do it," Joey offers wiping his blade off on Lance's shirt.

"No, we just need to bury him," Reno says in a definitive voice, everyone but Joey nodding in agreement.

They walk the slaughterhouse property to find a place to bury Charlie that will assure no one will ever be able to find him. They find a small gully overgrown with bushes north of the main building and decide that is the spot. Jeremy and Joey drag Charlie's lifeless body to his new grave while Reno and Lance look for shovels to dig the hole. They finish his grave just as the sun begins to set and when they are finished, they do not offer prayers. Instead, the boys each take turns pissing on it.

They find their way back to Carter's van, exhausted both mentally and physically and climb in. The van roars to life when Joey turns the key and begins their journey back home. During most of the trip, Lance's thoughts keep returning to Bear and he's glad the back of the van is dark so his friends don't see him cry, again. Even if they did, they would not say anything. None of them can blame him. Each of them already mourned for Bear in their own way.

CHAPTER 9

WHERE'S THE BEEF?

It's surreal; five teenagers and a little mutt dog saved the world.

When they get home, none of the parents were any wiser; they thought the kids ran off for a summertime adventure.

Reno was grounded for the rest of the summer vacation for stealing her sister's car, but it was returned unharmed.

Ryan's parents were ecstatic that he came home alive, and after hours and hours of debriefs by the police and FBI they concluded that Ryan was kidnapped by a traveling band of vagrant gypsy devil worshippers.

Nothing really happened to Lance, Jeremy, or Joey. They were scolded by their parents and allowed to enjoy the rest of their summer vacations.

All of them remembered what happened in Sheol and at home. They talked about it amongst themselves. They were their own quasi-support group and that would lead well into their adult lives.

Emma never did return, not even to say goodbye, and that hurt Lance, although he never brought it up.

The kids spent the rest of the summer swimming and boarding, keeping mostly to themselves. All of them swore off drinking, drugs, and even cussing, although Joey had a hard time with the last one.

At night Lance would cry himself to sleep thinking about Bear and how brave his little friend was to try and save Reno. By his bedside, he kept a picture of him holding Bear back when Bear was a puppy, and every night asked God to watch over him.

Bear's sacrifice was not lost on Reno. She also spent many a night thinking about Bear, hoping he was happy and safe in heaven with his favorite chew toy.

Lance and Reno would sneak out at night to be together. They mostly talked, but eventually they kissed, and in their small, private circle they were boyfriend and girlfriend.

It was the last night of summer vacation and Lance was having a hard time going to sleep. He was anxious about school the next day and also sad that his summer vacation was over. He lay in his bed tossing and turning and it was well past 11:00 p.m. when he heard a knock at the front door. At first, he assumed it was one of his mom's boyfriends so he didn't immediately get up to answer, but then he remembered his mom was out for the night. He was home alone. He dragged himself out of bed, worried about who would knock on the door this late. If it was one of his friends, they would have come to his window, not the door. His mind wandered and he was half expecting to see the police. Maybe his mom was hurt or in trouble, he was wide awake now.

"Who is it?" he asked quietly.

No answer.

Did I imagine I heard a knock? He thought just as it happened again, louder this time. *Nope, didn't imagine it.*

"Who is it?" he asked again, leaning into the door to try and hear.

"Lance, It's me, Emma."

Can it really be her?

He flings the door wide open and staring at him is Emma's beautiful face, and then he hears it…a bark. He looks down and Bear is scratching at his leg trying to climb up on him. Lance drops to his knees and immediately begins crying as he buries his face in his dog's mane.

It is Bear! Bear is alive.

Lance slid on his butt toward the couch still clutching Bear in his arms. Bear is frantically licking his face and ears as happy and overjoyed as Lance, even more.

"How, Emma? How did you bring Bear back?" Lance asked through the licks.

"Lance, my powers are limited, but I do have a few tricks up my sleeve," she said, sitting on the couch.

"Thank you, thank you, thank you so much! You don't know what this means to me," he said to her without looking at her, still focused on his furry friend.

"Oh, believe me, I do know. I'm just glad I could do it."

Lance eventually crawled up onto the couch.

"You don't know how much you mean to me, Emma. None of this could have been possible without you."

"No, none of this could have been possible without you and your friends. Do you realize what you've done, Lance?"

"Yeah, we talk about it from time to time, but none of it seems real. It seems like something made up."

"You're right in a way. No one other than us will ever believe it. Maybe that's for the best Lance, our secret."

"You're right. We've all sworn an oath to each other to never tell anyone else, not even our parents, or our wives when we get married."

"I think you will be able to talk to your wife about it." Emma had a feeling about Lance and Reno. She saw they were together for a very long time.

"What do you mean?" Lance didn't pick up on the clue and Emma didn't offer to explain.

"Nothing, just thinking out loud," she dismissed the conversation and directed it back to why she came to visit.

"Well, Lance, I'm here to say goodbye. You've come a long way and we've been through so much together that I felt it was only proper to say goodbye to you in person. And I wanted to see your face when you opened your door and saw Bear," she said to him, her hand on his shoulder now.

"What do you mean, goodbye? I thought we were together forever," he asked, confused.

"We are, we will always be together, just not like this anymore. My job is done and you have a whole life to live. You don't need me hanging around."

"Yes, yes, I do need you. You're my guardian angel. I need you."

"You don't. You're stronger than you've ever been and I said we're still going to be together. You just won't see or hear me anymore."

"I love you, Emma," Lance said, glancing up to look in her eyes. They made eye contact just as she was disappearing. She faded away as she was sitting on his couch, and then she was gone.

At first, Lance was sad, but he knew Emma would not want him to be. Every night when he said his prayers, he included her, his guardian angel, including tonight. He stood up and crawled into bed, Bear at his side, and he slept, a good restful sleep. He would be ready and refreshed for the first day of school.

Lance wakes up on the first blast of his clock/radio and jumps out of bed, Bear by his side. He still couldn't believe Bear was with him. He grins and picks him up, cradling him as he walks to the front door to let him out to go to the bathroom. He was sad that he had to leave the little guy alone while he was in school and wished he was able to stay home, but he knew that was not an option. He walks down to his little bathroom to get ready and then back to his bedroom to dress. He doesn't eat breakfast. His body was trained not to expect a morning meal, mostly because there usually wasn't food. His mom didn't buy him any new school clothes so he would be wearing a pair of his old jeans and a T-shirt. He let Bear back in and explained to him that he had to leave for a little bit, but would be home as soon as he can. Then he thought about Reno and how she would want to know about Bear. He glances up at the clock on the wall in the kitchen and decides he has enough time to take Bear to her house.

When Reno opens her door and Bear jumps up at her, her face lights up. She scoops Bear into her arms and begins crying. She walks over to the overstuffed Lazy-Boy recliner and plops down letting Bear shower her with kisses.

Looking up at Lance with disbelief she says, "Lance, how is this possible?"

"Don't ask me, Emma brought him back." He slides onto the couch next to her.

Hugging Bear and kissing his head she says, "Thank God, thank Emma. Lance you don't know how happy this makes me."

A feeling of relief washed over Reno when Bear jumped on her. She was being so hard on herself and she honestly thought the feeling of grief and guilt would never leave her.

"Well, I just wanted to bring him by to see you. He insisted."

"Thank you. This means the world to me. Tell Emma thank you for me, please."

"I'll bring him by after school and maybe we can go for a walk?"

Reno gave Bear back to Lance and said, "Of course." Her heart was filled with joy.

He put Bear back in his trailer and closed the door and began his walk to school meeting up with Jeremy, Joey, and Ryan. He didn't get a chance to tell them about Bear the night before so this would be his first opportunity.

"Guess what guys," Lance was excited to tell them all about Emma's visit.

"Let me guess...You're not a fucking virgin!" Joey yells as loudly as he can and then drops to one knee laughing as hard as he can, silently apologizing to himself in his head for cussing.

"No dork. I mean none of your business, but that's not what I was going to tell you guys."

"My bad, tell us please, we're all dying to hear what big, important news you have," Joey said.

Lance looked to Jeremy and Ryan and they both nodded their heads but didn't really look interested. "Okay then, Be—" he spat out before he was interrupted once again.

Turning the corner was Larry and his gang. Before summer vacation, the sight of Larry barreling down on him would send Lance into shock, but not anymore. Lance waited for them to catch up and courageously stepped forward to greet Larry.

"Hi Larry, how was your summer vacation?"

Larry looked at Lance with a tinge of shock that the skinny little punk walked up to him like that, like they're friends. "Bitch, please, you better step back."

Larry directed his attention to Jeremy who he felt was at least vaguely on the same level as him. "Didn't see you at any of my parties, what happened? They were dope."

"Yeah, we were kind of busy this summer with other stuff," was the only response Jeremy offered.

"Too busy to get wasted and be knee-deep in girls that want to party?" Larry asked with a look of shock and disbelief.

Everything in Larry's life revolved around drugs and girls. He didn't think you were normal if those two things were not your top priority.

"Yep, too busy, but I heard about some of them. My brother said he went to one and it was dope."

"Damn right. I remember seeing Brian. The girls couldn't keep from falling all over him. Damn to be that good looking," Larry said, looking at Jeremy with an expression of *What happened to you? You sleeping when they were passing out good looks?*

Larry thought he was God's gift to women, but it was the parties and drugs that he always has readily available that made the girls like him and everyone but him knew that.

Frankie, one of Larry's buddies, puffed up to Lance. "Hey little bitch, what were you guys doing that was more important than one of Larry's parties?"

Lance and basically everyone felt sorry for Frankie. He had one cock-eye that was blue and brown and his eyes always looked like they were bulging out of his head, but he was mean and very strong for his size so no one ever brought it up.

There was a high schooler that was teasing Frankie at the bowling alley last year and Frankie sent him to the hospital to get his jaw wired shut.

"Get off me, Frankie. I'm not afraid of you," Lance said, thinking in his head, *You realize I could literally melt you right where you stand.*

"Oh no, you didn't. You didn't just tell me to fuck off," Frankie exclaimed, raising his fists preparing for a quick fight.

All of the other kids crowded around Frankie and Lance including Larry, egging them on.

Frankie's friends started chanting, "Where's the beef, bitches? Where's the beef? Frankie is getting ready to pound your dog face into hamburger!"

Jeremy, Joey, and Ryan stepped back and didn't say a word. They knew what Lance could do.

Frankie threw a haphazard punch directed at Lance's nose. Lance sidestepped and grabbed Frankie's fist. He could squeeze and break every bone in Frankie's hand but decided to give him a chance and released it. Frankie was furious. He threw some sort of karate kick followed up by a wide-wielding roundhouse punch. He missed. Lance slapped Frankie in the face so hard it knocked him out. Frankie's legs gave out and he slumped down onto the street, asleep. Everyone looked in disbelief and Larry decided he needed to finish what Frankie couldn't. He cracked his knuckles giving Lance all the warning he needed that he was getting ready to pounce. Lance swung at Larry first. And with his other hand gestured toward him. The illusion was that Lance just hit Larry so hard he flew back about ten feet and landed on his ass. Everyone watching lets out a string of swearing.

"Oh shit!"

"That didn't just happen."

"Lance knocked Larry the fuck out!"

Larry sat up, shocked and confused, but conscious enough to know that he didn't want any more of that. He scrambled to his feet and without a word turned around and started running away, his buddies closely following behind him.

At the same time, Lance, Jeremy, Joey, and Ryan yelled, "WHERE'S THE BEEF, BITCHES?"

They laughed aloud and then apologized to each other for cussing.

The rest of the school year was amazing, one for the ages. The super-secret superhero gang had an amazing year.

S T A Y   S C A R E D !